Penguin

THE THURSDAY MURDER CLUB

RICHARD OSMAN

LEVEL

RETOLD BY ANNA TREWIN
ILLUSTRATED BY ALAN BROWN
SERIES EDITOR: SORREL PITTS

Contains adult content, which could include: sexual behaviour or exploitation, misuse of alcohol, smoking, illegal drugs, violence and dangerous behaviour.

This book includes content that may be distressing to readers, including descriptions of suicide or self-harm, abusive or discriminatory treatment of individuals, groups, religions or communities.

PENGUIN BOOKS

UK | USA | Canada | Ireland | Australia
India | New Zealand | South Africa

Penguin Books is part of the Penguin Random House group of companies
whose addresses can be found at global.penguinrandomhouse.com.
www.penguin.co.uk www.puffin.co.uk www.ladybird.co.uk

The Thursday Murder Club first published by Viking, 2020
Published by Penguin Books 2021
This Penguin Readers edition published by Penguin Books Ltd, 2025
001

Original text written by Richard Osman
Text for Penguin Readers edition adapted by Anna Trewin

Illustrated by Alan Brown
Jacket lettering by Joel Holland

Cover design by Penguin Books Ltd

Printed and bound in Great Britain by Clays Ltd, Elcograf S.p.A.

The authorized representative in the EEA is Penguin Random House Ireland,
Morrison Chambers, 32 Nassau Street, Dublin D02 YH68

A CIP catalogue record for this book is available from the British Library

ISBN: 978–0–241–70063–1

All correspondence to:
Penguin Books
Penguin Random House Children's
One Embassy Gardens, 8 Viaduct Gardens,
London SW11 7BW

Contents

Note about the story

Richard Osman is a famous British writer, and he has also had a long career on British TV, where he introduces popular game shows. *The Thursday Murder Club* (now part of a crime series) is his first novel.

The story is about a group of **pensioners*** who call themselves the "Thursday Murder Club" because they meet on Thursdays to try to **solve** old murder cases. The pensioners live in a very comfortable **retirement** village in Kent, an area in the south-east of England.

The police in the story all have job titles that tell you their level of ability. Chris Hudson, who is the leader of his team, is a Detective Chief Inspector (DCI). This is a higher level than Penny Gray, who was a Detective Inspector (DI), and Donna De Freitas, who is a Police Constable (PC). Police Constable is the starting job in policing.

Priests usually have the word "Father" before their names, so one of the **suspects**, Matthew Mackie, is called Father Matthew Mackie.

Before-reading questions

1 Read the "Note about the story". What would it be like to live in a retirement village like Coopers Chase, do you think?

2 How are old people in your country treated? Do they live with their families or in other special places? Are they respected and cared for enough, do you think?

*Definitions of words in **bold** can be found in the glossary on pages 108–111.

CHAPTER ONE
The Thursday Murder Club

Joyce

It started with Elizabeth. She lives with her husband Stephen in one of the nice three-bedroom apartments in Larkin Court. I was having lunch in our "modern ***upscale*** *restaurant" and Elizabeth came over and said she was sorry because she could see I was eating, but could she ask me a question about knife wounds. I said, "No problem," so she put a file on the table and I saw the edges of some old photographs. Then she asked me to imagine that someone had* ***stabbed*** *a girl with a knife maybe three or four times in the chest – in and out very quickly, but without cutting an* ***artery****. How long would it take the girl to die? I replied that the girl would probably die in about forty-five minutes.*

I should mention now that my name is Joyce Meadowcroft – the Meadowcroft came from my husband, Gerry (he's dead now and I miss him a lot, but I don't talk about him that much). I was a nurse for many years, and that's why Elizabeth was asking me. Sorry, I've only just started writing this diary. I'll get better at it, I promise.

"But what if she was helped?" replied Elizabeth. "Not by a doctor, but anyone who could cover the wound and stop the blood?"

"Well, then she wouldn't die at all," I replied. Elizabeth nodded and said she had said the same to Ibrahim, although I didn't know Ibrahim at that time. This was all a couple of months ago.

I was glad to help Elizabeth and asked if there was any way I could look at the picture of the body. Elizabeth took out a photo, passed it to me face-down, and smiled.

"Can I ask you one more question?" she said.

"Of course," I replied.

"Are you ever free on Thursdays?"

And that was when I first got invited to the Thursday Murder Club – and decided to keep a diary about it. The club was Elizabeth, Ibrahim Arif, who lives in Wordsworth Court, and Ron Ritchie – yes, the famous Ron Ritchie from the ***trade unions****. I found out that he lived in the village from a story about him in the Coopers Chase newsletter,* Cut to the Chase. *Ron and John Gray had found an injured* ***fox*** *and nursed it back to health. They'd called it Scargill after the famous trade union leader. As John had once been a* ***vet****, I* ***suspected*** *that he had done the nursing and Ron had just chosen the name.*

John Gray's wife, Penny, also used to be part of the club, but she's in Willows now. That's the village's ***nursing home*** *– where* ***residents*** *move when they are too old or ill to live in the apartments. I suppose when she moved there, it created a space, and I became the new Penny.*

Elizabeth and Penny had started the club. Penny had been a Detective Inspector in the Kent Police for many years, and she had a file of ***unsolved*** *murder cases. I'm not allowed to say what Elizabeth's job was, but I know that murders and* ***investigations*** *would not be new to her.*

Anyway, Penny, Elizabeth, Ibrahim and Ron met every Thursday in the ***Jigsaw*** *Room and went through the files looking for anything that the police had missed. They didn't want to think that there were guilty people still out there. The club was also good fun – a glass of wine, biscuits and a mystery.*

But I must stop writing now. There's a big ***consultation*** *tomorrow* *about a new development here at Coopers Chase. Ian Ventham, the owner, is coming to talk to us. I have to be honest – I don't like him. He's all the things that can go wrong with a man. I know that Ron is planning to cause a lot of trouble, and I'm looking forward to watching him do that.*

PC Donna De Freitas would like to have a gun and be catching murderers. But as she sits down for lunch at 11:45 in the morning with four **pensioners** she has only just met, 26-year-old Donna understands that she will have to work her way up to all that. And, actually, the last hour, giving her talk on "Home Safety", has been quite fun after so much paperwork. Fairhaven Police Station is sleepier than she is used to. Her last job was with the Metropolitan Police in London, but she had to leave it. For a moment, she wonders what her ex, Carl, is doing now – probably trying to find a girlfriend on a **dating app**. But Donna does not want to think about that.

Today, she has come to Coopers Chase **Retirement** Village, a very pleasant group of apartments that sit in a large area of woodland near Fairhaven in Kent. The village seems to have everything – Donna has seen signs to an exercise room and library, as well as the huge residents' lounge where she gave her talk. An old **convent** and its **chapel** sit in the centre of the development; its west side includes a swimming pool, a **sauna** and gym. Next to the convent is Willows, the village's nursing home. Above the buildings, the pensioners tell her, a path runs through a tunnel of trees up a hill to the metal-gated **cemetery**, where the convent **nuns** sleep forever.

There are about 300 pensioners living here, and it is different to what Donna had expected. Because as soon as she had started her talk, a smartly-dressed woman in her eighties in the front row stood up and said, "I'm Elizabeth. No window locks please, and don't tell us not to give our bank details to strangers over the phone. We know all that." And lots of heads nodded.

"Well, what shall we talk about then?" asked Donna.

"I'd like to discuss police mistakes," said a man with a West Ham United **tattoo** on his neck. "When they arrest, or shoot, the wrong people."

"Sit down, Ron!" said the smart lady.

And so it went on, enjoyably, until the hour was finished and they had thanked Donna warmly and invited her to lunch. So here she is, eating a very tasty salad in what the menu calls a "modern upscale restaurant". She notices the pensioners are eating huge platefuls and have also opened a bottle of red wine.

"That really was wonderful, Donna," says Elizabeth.

"It was great," says Ron.

"I would be a good **drug smuggler**, I think." This was Ibrahim, who Donna had learned used to be a psychiatrist. He wore a nice suit with a handkerchief in his pocket. "They have modern machines now to count the money. Guess how old I am, PC De Freitas."

Donna looks at Ibrahim's hands – they always tell the truth.

"Eighty?" she says, and sees the wind leave Ibrahim's sails.

"Yes, exactly," he says, "but I look about seventy-four. Everyone agrees. The secret is lots of yoga."

"And what's your story, Joyce?" asks Donna to the fourth member of the group, a small white-haired woman in a blue blouse who smiles a lot.

"Me?" says Joyce. "No story. I was a nurse and a mother. My daughter is the interesting one in the family. She manages a **financial** company in London."

A question has been pulling at Donna, and she decides to ask it. "So, how did you become friends?"

"Friends?" Elizabeth smiles. "Oh, we're not friends."

Ron laughs. "No, we're not friends. More wine, Liz?"

Elizabeth nods and Ron pours. They are on their second bottle now. It is 12:15.

Ibrahim agrees. "We're interested in different things. I like Ron, but, being an ex-trade union leader, he can be difficult."

Ron nods.

"And Elizabeth can be quite cold."

Elizabeth agrees. "That's true. I've never been easy to like."

"I think we *all* like Joyce," says Ibrahim.

Ron and Elizabeth nod together this time.

Donna stares at them in confusion. "So, if you're not friends, then what are you?"

Joyce looks up and laughs. "Well," she says. "Firstly, we are friends. This lot are just a bit slow to realize it. And secondly, I'm sorry if we didn't say it when we invited you. We're the Thursday Murder Club."

CHAPTER TWO
The consultation

Ian Ventham parks his Range Rover in the disabled space, not because he has a problem walking but because it is close to the door. Then he walks through Waitrose supermarket to the café where Bogdan is waiting for him.

For a few minutes, they argue about payment for a swimming pool that Bogdan has recently **tiled**. They had agreed four **grand** for the work, but now Ian only wants to pay two. Finally, Bogdan, tiring of Ventham's arguments, says he will accept three.

Ian hands the money over. "It's actually two grand eight hundred," he says. "But that's close enough for friends. Now, I wanted to ask you about something."

"Sure," says Bogdan, putting the money in his pocket.

"You seem like an intelligent man."

Bogdan smiles and shakes his head. "Well, I speak very good Polish. My English not perfect though."

"When I ask you to do a job, it gets done well, and cheaply," says Ventham. "I'm on my way to **fire** Tony Curran. And I need someone to take his place. Would you like that?"

For the next few minutes, Bogdan listens to Ventham's idea. After he's finished, the Pole smiles.

"Too much for you?" asks Ventham.

"No, I can do the job. But if you fire Tony, maybe he kills you."

Ian finishes his tea. "I know, but let me worry about that. And tomorrow the job's all yours."

"Sure, if you're alive," replies Bogdan.

Ron Ritchie, as usual, is having none of it. He is standing up and pointing at a document. His finger is shaking but his voice is still strong, and he feels pleased to have something to be angry about again. Back in the old days, they used to call him "Red Ron". He had organized hundreds of trade union walkouts – in companies and at factories and shipping ports. Anyone who had ever needed to be defended was always safe in Ron's **tattooed** arms.

"Now, here's a sentence, and it's in your words, Mr Ventham, not mine," he continues. "Coopers Chase Holding Investments has the right to develop further in consultation with the residents."

"But this is a consultation meeting," says Ian Ventham, as if talking to a child. "You're the residents. You can **consult** as much as you like for the next twenty minutes."

Ian sits at a table in front of the residents. His skin is brown from the sun, and his sunglasses are pushed up over his hair. He wears an expensive shirt and a watch as big as a clock. On one side of him sits a young woman – the development architect – and on the other, a man with lots of tattoos. Ron thinks it must be Tony Curran, Ventham's builder, who he has heard about.

"You're calling it 'The Woodlands'," says Ron, "when you're planning to cut down all the trees. You have your nice computer pictures, but what we want to see is a proper **model** – with trees and little people."

Everyone claps. A lot of people wanted to see a model, but Ventham said it was not done these days.

"You know where you can put this document, don't you?" Ron shouts at Ventham, feeling happy. He is back in the fight and there is nothing like it.

As Father Matthew Mackie enters the back of the residents' lounge, a large man in a football shirt is shouting. There are many people here, as Mackie had hoped. He takes a biscuit and sits in the back row. The man in the football shirt has sat down now, and other people are speaking. Father Mackie pushes his hand through his snowy-white hair. How strange it is to be in this room. He **shivers**. It's probably just the cold.

The consultation is over. Ron is sitting with Joyce in the garden of Coopers Chase, drinking cold beers in the sunshine. His son, Jason, who has come to visit, is sitting with them. Jason used to be a successful **boxer**, but he's a television **celebrity** now.

"Joyce said she saw you on a cooking programme last week," says Ron. "Are you really doing *Celebrity Ice Dance* as well?"

"I thought it might be fun," says Jason.

Ron drinks a mouthful of his beer then looks over Jason's shoulder. "Over by the BMW, Jason – that's Ventham."

Jason slowly turns his head. "And that's Curran talking to

him," adds his father. "Have you ever seen him in town?"

"Once or twice," says Jason.

The conversation between Ventham and Curran does not look happy. They move their hands angrily, and they speak fast and low.

"Looks like they're arguing," says Ron.

Jason drinks some of his beer and watches the men carefully.

"Want a game of cards this afternoon?" his father asks.

"Sorry, Dad, but I've got something to do this afternoon."

Jason leaves, and Ron watches him a little worriedly. There is something not right with his son today.

Ian Ventham is happy about the consultation. He was not worried about the loud man with the tattoos, or the **priest**. "That priest must be worried about the cemetery," thinks Ian. "Well, let him try and stop me."

Ian is already thinking ahead. After The Woodlands, there will be a final stage to the development, Hillcrest. He has driven the five minutes up a rough track from Coopers Chase and is now sitting in Karen Playfair's kitchen. Her father, Gordon, owns the land at the top of the hill, and he does not want to sell. It does not worry Ventham, who has his ways.

"I'm afraid nothing has changed," says Karen. "Dad won't sell, and I can't make him."

"I understand," says Ventham. "More money."

"No. And I think you know this already. He just doesn't like you."

Gordon Playfair had taken one look at Ian Ventham and disappeared upstairs. Ian knows that sometimes people did not like him, but he has learned to live with it. It was their problem.

"But leave it with me," says Karen. "I'll find a way."

Karen Playfair understands Ian Ventham. He has been explaining to her how much money she could make if she could get her father to sell. As Ventham stares at her in her big jumper, he wonders when she gave up on life. Ventham is on lots of dating apps and keeps a top age of 25 for the women he wants to **date**. Karen must be 50 – the same age as him. "It's different for a woman, though," he thinks. But if he has to be nice to a 50-year-old woman for a few weeks, then he can do it.

As he shakes her hand and leaves, he realizes that the only woman over 25 that he spends any time at all with is his wife.

"Oh well," he thinks. "Time to go. Things to do."

Tony Curran makes his decision as he stops his BMW in front of his house. He is going to kill Ian Ventham with a gun he keeps under a tree in his garden. If he can remember which tree. There is only so much any man can take. Curran begins to sing to himself as he goes into the huge house he bought eighteen months ago with the money he has made from Coopers Chase. He switches off the expensive alarm that Ventham had some men put in last week – Polish guys, but then everyone in the UK was Polish these days.

Curran's wife is not back yet, but that's fine. He needs time to think and plan. Slowly, he goes back over the argument with Ventham he'd had earlier that afternoon. Ventham had fired him. And it was so quickly done – just a conversation on the way back to his car. He had wanted to hit Ventham, but he knew better. He kept the argument small and quiet so that when Ventham is found dead, no one can say they saw him and Tony Curran shouting at each other.

Curran sits down at the kitchen table. Nothing needed to be done tonight. Let the world continue, keep the birds singing in the garden, and then do it. Why did anyone cause trouble for Tony Curran? When had that ever gone well for them?

Tony hears the noise a second too late. He turns to see the huge **spanner** as it comes towards him. In the short second he has before he dies, he understands. "You can't always win, Tony. That's only fair."

The spanner hits him above the eye, and he falls to the floor. The birds in the garden stop singing for a second, and then continue.

The killer puts a photograph on the table as Tony Curran's fresh blood makes a wide pool around his head.

CHAPTER THREE
The investigation begins

"I have a job for you," says Elizabeth, after arriving at Ibrahim's apartment very early. She had rung him the night before with the news about Tony Curran. She had heard it from Ron, who had heard it from Jason, who had heard it from an unknown **source**. "All I need you to do is lie to a police officer," she continues. "Can I trust you to do that?"

"When can you not trust me, Elizabeth?" asks Ibrahim.

"So, who killed Tony Curran and how do we catch him, or her?" asks Elizabeth.

After visiting Ibrahim, she had immediately come to see Penny.

"I'm sure he has enemies," Elizabeth continues. She is sitting in her usual chair near Penny's bed. "More tattoos than Ron, big house, etc. Why don't we start by looking at Ian Ventham? He and Tony Curran had a little argument – Ron and Joyce saw them. Perhaps Ventham is unhappy with Curran and they have something to discuss. But they do it outside where people can see them. Why? Because Ventham has to give him bad news, and he's frightened of how Curran will react. He hopes to make Curran calm, but he's unsuccessful – this is Ron's idea."

There is a small **sponge** next to the bed. Elizabeth puts it in a bowl of water and wipes Penny's dry lips.

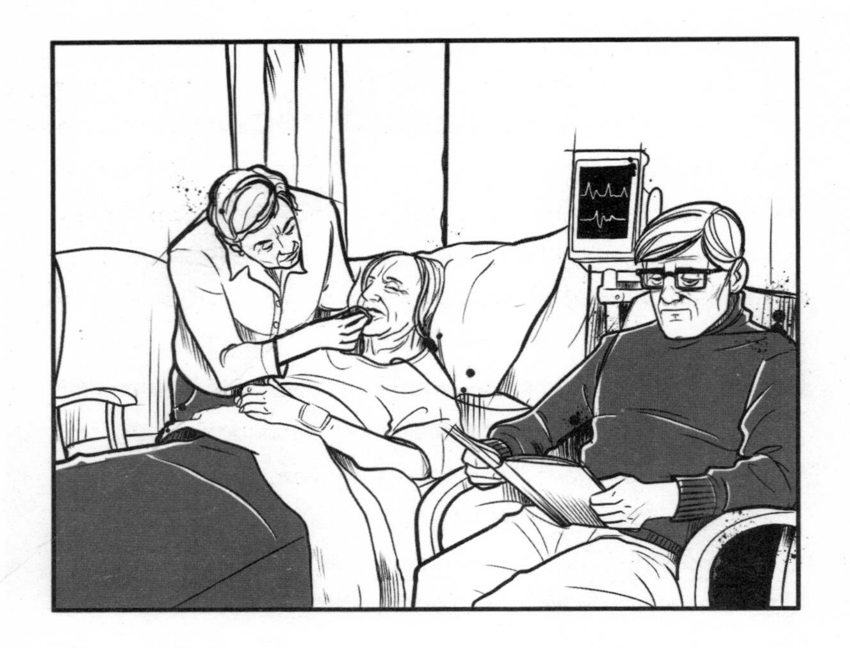

"What would Ventham do in that situation, Penny? Follow Curran to his house? Kill Curran before Curran kills him? I want to know about their financial relationship. There's a man in Geneva who owes me a favour, so we should be able to get Ventham's financial files by this evening."

Elizabeth stands and kisses her friend on the top of her head, then smiles at Penny's husband, who is sitting on the other side of her.

"How are you, John?"

He puts down his book and looks up.

"Oh, you know . . ."

"I do," Elizabeth replies.

The nurses say Penny Gray can hear nothing, but who can really know? John never speaks to Penny when Elizabeth is in the room. He comes to Willows at seven each morning and leaves at nine each evening to go back to the apartment that he and Penny had shared.

Elizabeth leaves the lovers together.

Donna carries tea into the **incident** room, which is full of police officers. A builder from Fairhaven has been murdered, and DCI Chris Hudson is talking to his team. "There's **CCTV** at the house," he tells them. "Tony Curran left Coopers Chase at 2 p.m. and he died at 3:32 – we know that from his broken watch. That's not a lot of time to search."

Donna has placed the tea on a desk. She reaches down, **pretending** to tie her shoe. She's interested to hear Chris mention Coopers Chase.

"There are also traffic cameras on the roads near the house. So let's get those videos, too," says Chris. "Are you all right, Constable?"

"Yes, sir," Donna replies, straightening and moving towards the door.

"Until we can look at the CCTV," Chris continues, "our best lead is the photograph the killer left by the body. Let's have a look at it."

Donna turns and sees lit on the wall an old photograph of three men in a pub laughing and drinking. Their table is covered in money. She only has a moment, but she recognizes one of them immediately.

"Constable?" says Chris, moving his eyes towards the door.

"Sorry, sir," she replies, and walks through, back to more boring paperwork.

"So, we know these three men very well," continues Chris. "Shall we talk about them one by one?"

The door shuts and Donna **sighs**.

Later that day, the phone on Donna's desk rings. "There are two old ladies here, and one of them says someone has stolen her bag," says the receptionist. "She's a nun, and she'll only talk to a female police officer."

When Donna reaches reception, she is surprised to see Elizabeth and Joyce there. She immediately takes them to an **interview** room. They all sit down.

"So, you're a nun now, are you, Elizabeth?" Donna asks.

Elizabeth smiles and takes out a notebook as Joyce looks around the room. "This is exactly like you see on TV, PC De Freitas. It must be such fun to work here!"

Donna, however, is not smiling. "Can I ask what the two of you are doing here before I go back to catching **criminals**?"

Elizabeth claps her hands lightly. "Firstly, stop pretending you're not pleased to see us. And secondly, we know you're not catching criminals." She looks down at her notebook. "We know you left the Metropolitan Police and came from London to

Fairhaven – probably because of a relationship that went wrong – and you're very bored. Most of the officers here are older than you, and you feel you've made a mistake. But you wait and hope something exciting will happen – like a woman who isn't a nun pretending that her bag has been stolen."

Donna's face does not change. "What are you doing here, Elizabeth?" she repeats.

"Wouldn't you like to be **investigating** the Tony Curran murder?"

Donna rests her chin on her hands. "There's already a team investigating the murder. I just took them their tea in the incident room."

"They say he was hit with a large spanner," says Elizabeth, looking down at her notes. "Is that true?"

"I can't say."

"Wouldn't you like to be part of it, Donna?"

Donna looks down at the table. "OK, yes, I would very much like to be part of it. But I can't just ask because I'm bored."

Elizabeth smiles. "Don't worry about that. We can organize it."

"You can organize it?" says Donna. "How? And when?"

Elizabeth looks at her watch and smiles. "In an hour, maybe?"

"And this conversation never leaves this room?" asks Donna.

Elizabeth lifts a finger to her lips.

Donna holds up her hands. "But what will you get out of it?"

"We're just helping a new friend," says Elizabeth. "And we

may occasionally have a question for you."

"You know I can't tell you anything that's **confidential**?"

Elizabeth nods. "Nothing confidential. As a woman of God, I promise."

"In an hour, you say?"

Elizabeth looks at her watch. "Yes, depending on the traffic."

DCI Chris Hudson is sitting with Ibrahim and Ron in Ibrahim's comfortable apartment. After the surprise of seeing Coopers Chase – he has been to retirement villages before, and this lovely, peaceful development is not what he was expecting – he is even more surprised to see Ron Ritchie, the famous trade union leader and father of Jason Ritchie, whom Chris is investigating. Chris thinks again about the three men in the photo. Tony Curran and Bobby Tanner, arms around each other. And to the side, a bottle in his hand and that handsome broken nose, Jason Ritchie.

But what had happened to angry Red Ron? He is wearing old **pyjamas** and no shoes, and looking around with empty eyes.

"It can be very stressful for old people to talk to the police," Ibrahim explains, after making them all tea. "Ron really wants to talk to you about the argument he saw."

"I just . . . don't think . . . I can," says Ron. "I don't . . . want . . . any trouble."

"I promise there won't be any trouble," says Chris. "You can tell me anything, and it will stay confidential."

"I think . . . I think I'd be happier talking to the lady . . ."

Chris turns to Ibrahim. "The lady?"

"The lady who came . . . to talk to us about . . . home safety," says Ron.

"Oh, yes!" says Ibrahim. "PC De Freitas. Do you know her, DCI Hudson?"

"Of course, she's one of my team." Chris tries to remember if the young woman who brought in the tea was Donna De Freitas. "But she's not working on this case."

Ron and Ibrahim don't say a word. They just look quietly at Chris.

"But it's a great idea," says Chris. "I'll bring her in on the case."

Ron picks up his cup of tea for the first time. "That would be good. I'll talk to Jason."

"Jason?" asks Chris.

"My son, Jason Ritchie, the boxer. He was here and saw the argument, too."

CHAPTER FOUR
To London and back

Joyce

So, this has been an unexpected day. I was just having my hair cut by a handsome young man when Elizabeth arrived. She told me a taxi was coming and I should get ready for a day out in London. I didn't ask any questions and we were soon on the train. By the time we got to Tunbridge Wells, Elizabeth couldn't keep it a secret any more. We were going to see my daughter, Joanna! Elizabeth had emailed her and asked if she would look at the financial records of Ian Ventham's companies. She'd also told Joanna not to discuss it with me so it would be a nice surprise. Which it was, of course.

We took a black cab from Charing Cross station to Joanna's beautiful offices in Mayfair. When we arrived, she was waiting for us, and it was lovely to see her. She even gave me a hug, and when Elizabeth went to use the bathroom, Joanna smiled and said, "Mum! A murder?" She looked like the child I remembered from long ago.

We sat in a huge meeting room with a long, shining wooden table. Elizabeth had already emailed over the files, and Joanna had given them to Cornelius, who works for her. He's an ***expert*** *at what he does and has found two very interesting things that we'll be telling the police.*

I've talked to Elizabeth about Joanna before, about how we were not as close as other mothers and daughters. Elizabeth knew that I'd been feeling a bit sad about this, and I wondered if the trip had really been for me, because many people could tell us what Cornelius has told us.

Later, Elizabeth and I went for a walk around Mayfair, and then we drank wine on the train home. I think this murder thing is going to be lots of fun.

Donna had received the news yesterday morning – she was now on the Tony Curran murder case. Chris Hudson had given her the file, and she had read about how Curran had once been involved in a shooting at a pub in Fairhaven called the Black Bridge. Someone had shot a young drug dealer. Then the only **witness** to the crime, a taxi driver, disappeared. At that time, Curran ran the drugs business in Fairhaven and was making a lot of money. The police had spoken to him many times about the shooting, but he had refused to answer any of their questions.

And then, since 2000, the only **criminal** incident recorded for Tony Curran had been a speeding ticket, quickly paid, in 2009.

Tony Curran had simply **got away with** murder before being murdered himself, Donna thinks as she and Chris Hudson park in front of Ian Ventham's huge house. A few minutes later, they are in his enormous living room and showing him the photograph that was left by Curran's body.

"No, I'm certain I've never seen it," Ventham says. "I recognize poor Tony though, and that's Jason Ritchie, the boxer, isn't it?"

Chris nods as Donna looks around Ventham's living room. With its bright red piano and gold chairs, it is one of the strangest rooms she has ever seen. On the wall is a huge painting of

Ventham carrying a sword.

"My **boxing** trainer once said I could be a successful boxer," says Ventham. "With my brain and body – there's some things you can't teach."

"Did you and Tony have an argument?" interrupts Chris. "Before he died?"

"An argument – me and Tony?" asks Ian, slowly.

"Yes," says Chris. "I've got three witnesses who saw the two of you arguing."

Ventham puts his hand under his chin. "We had an argument, sure. It was about water **sprinklers**. I wanted to put them in the new apartments. Tony didn't want to. Fire safety was always more important to me than Tony. So, yes, we argued about the sprinklers, but it was only a small thing."

Chris nods and turns to Donna. "I think we're finished for now, Mr Ventham," he says. "Or do you have any questions, PC De Freitas?"

"Just one thing," Donna says. "Where did you go after you left Coopers Chase that day? Did you come home? Or did you visit Tony Curran to continue discussing the sprinklers?"

"I did neither," says Ventham. "I drove up the hill and met with Karen and Gordon Playfair. They'll tell you the same. You're very beautiful, by the way, PC De Freitas – for a police officer."

"You'll see how beautiful I am if I ever have to arrest you," replies Donna.

As they are walking back to the car, Donna's phone suddenly **pings**. It's a text from Elizabeth.

"The Thursday Murder Club are asking if we'll come over to Coopers Chase, sir. They have some information."

"The Thursday Murder Club?" asks Chris.

"That's what they call themselves. Elizabeth says that Jason Ritchie will be there."

Chris Hudson is sitting uncomfortably on a two-person sofa in Joyce's living room, between Ibrahim and Joyce. He has a cup of tea in one hand and a plate of Joyce's lemon cake in the other, but his arms are so pressed in that it is difficult to eat or drink. Opposite him sits a terrifying woman called Elizabeth, a much younger-looking Ron Ritchie, and Donna, who seems very relaxed in an armchair.

"As you know, myself and PC De Freitas are investigating the murder of a builder called Tony Curran," Chris tells the group. "I know you and Joyce were having a drink with your son, Mr Ritchie, and saw an argument between Tony Curran and Ian Ventham. I understand Jason may be joining us?"

"He just texted," says Ron. "He'll be ten minutes. So have you got fingerprints or **DNA**?"

Chris remembers Ron being much more confused than this the other day. Elizabeth watches him. "You look uncomfortable. Why don't you move to another chair?" she says.

Chris happily moves from the sofa.

"And do you have any **suspects**?" she says.

"I'm afraid that is information I can't really share," replies Chris.

"So, you *do* have a suspect. Oh, how wonderful! What do you think of the lemon cake?" says Joyce. "*I* made it."

"It's lovely," says Chris.

"Well, I feel this meeting has been all give and no take," says Elizabeth, and hands him a thick blue file. "You might like to look at this. It's some financial information about Ian Ventham. Details of this place, his relationship with Tony Curran and the twelve million he made from his death. You'll see that Curran had **shares** in Coopers Chase, and the documents show that these shares would go back to Ian Ventham if Curran were to die."

At that moment, Joyce's doorbell rings and she goes out. She returns with a younger man, and Chris immediately recognizes the tattooed arms and famous nose. Jason Ritchie, the great boxer and now famous TV celebrity. Between the two careers, though, Chris knew that there had been a time when Jason had made his money a different way. That was when he was photographed with Tony Curran and the other man, a drug dealer called Bobby Tanner. These were the years that Chris and Donna were interested in.

"Mr Ritchie," says Chris, shaking his hand. "We meet at last."

Chris wants a photo of himself with the famous celebrity, so he, Jason and Donna go outside where the light is better. Both men smile for the camera.

"So, I wanted to know what you're thinking," says Chris. "About Tony Curran. You must have known him a bit, from around Fairhaven?"

"Not really," says Jason. "He had a lot of enemies."

"You never drank with him in the Black Bridge pub – the one near the station? Maybe twenty years ago?"

For a second, Jason is still, then he quickly replies, "Perhaps. I'll think about it. If I do remember anything, I'll tell you."

"I saw a photo recently," says Chris. "You, Tony Curran and a man called Bobby Tanner. All very friendly."

"Lots of strangers ask me for photos," says Jason, turning to Donna. "Would you text me a copy of the one you just took?"

She takes his number, knowing this is his way of trying to get hers. He's not going to have it.

"And we can't find Bobby Tanner," says Chris. "Do you know where he is?"

Jason Ritchie quickly presses his lips together and shakes his head.

CHAPTER FIVE
Screw it. Let's do it.

Elizabeth goes straight to Willows after meeting with the police. John is in his usual chair, reading a book. Elizabeth reports everything to Penny and then adds, "Maybe Ventham isn't a suspect. Maybe those shares in Coopers Chase have made us blind. I mean, where was Ventham when Curran was killed? Was it even possible for him to do it?"

"Elizabeth, sorry," says John, suddenly, looking up. "But have you ever watched *Escape to the Country*?"

Elizabeth is not used to John speaking. "I don't think I have," she replies, "no."

"It's all about couples moving to the countryside. Anyway, I was watching it on the day that Curran was killed, and they'd just got to the end. I looked out of the window, and I saw Ventham's car, driving away down the hill. *Escape to the Country* finishes at 3."

"Thank you, John." Elizabeth takes out her phone. "Now, I need to send a text message."

A few minutes later, Elizabeth receives Donna's reply to her question.

> Curran died at 3:32. His watch broke when he fell.

It is early morning at the police station, and Chris Hudson's murder team are drinking coffee as Chris tells them what he has learned from the Thursday Murder Club.

"We know that Ian Ventham, Tony Curran's business partner, fired Curran less than two hours before the murder. Curran was going to lose a lot of money, and his death has made Ventham even more money. Over twelve million. The two men were seen having an argument just before Curran returned home. Did Ventham follow him? We know that Curran was killed at 3:32 last Tuesday, but when did Ventham leave Coopers Chase that day?" He turns to a young officer. "Where are we on traffic cameras, Terry? Have you got Ventham's **registration number**?"

"I've got the number, but it's not come up on any cameras yet," replies DI Terry Hallet, whose slim, strong body makes Chris think guiltily about his own love of chocolate and chips.

"And where are we with the other man in the photograph, Bobby Tanner?"

"We've talked to the police in Amsterdam," says a DI. "Tanner worked there after the Black Bridge shooting, but then he disappeared."

"It would be good to chat with him, if only to **rule** him **out**. Anything else?"

A young officer puts up her hand. "I've been looking at Tony Curran's phone records. He got three calls on the morning of the murder, but he didn't answer any of them – all from the same mobile number."

Chris nods. "Good work, Granger. Email me everything you've got."

"Of course, sir."

"OK, let's get back to it," finishes Chris. "Keep looking for Bobby Tanner. Someone must know where he is."

Donna's phone pings. It's a text from Elizabeth.

Good luck with the meeting today. We are having a little Thursday Murder Club road trip, if you have any information to give us. Oh, and my sources saw Chris buying chocolate biscuits this morning. You lucky thing. Also, Joyce says hello.

The morning sun is bright in the Kent sky. Ibrahim, Elizabeth, Joyce and Ron are all sitting in Ron's car, but Ibrahim is driving because he's the only one who understands Google Maps.

They are parked outside Tony Curran's gate. It was close, Ibrahim tells them after many minutes of writing down numbers and concentrating hard, but yes, there had been enough time for Ian Ventham to kill Tony Curran. If Ventham had left Coopers Chase at 3 p.m. and driven fast, he would have arrived at Tony Curran's huge house at 3:29. That gave him two minutes to get out of his car, get into the house, and hit Tony Curran with a spanner.

Ian Ventham is running in his gym and listening to Richard Branson's book *Screw It, Let's Do It: Lessons in Life and Business*. One day, Ian will write a book. He just needs a good title, and then he will start work.

As he runs, he's thinking about the cemetery and the priest he had seen at the consultation. Ventham does not want any trouble. If he hadn't fired Tony, he might have asked him to visit the priest, but Tony has gone, and Ian doesn't want to think about that any more. Richard Branson would move on, and so will Ian.

The digging is going to start in a week. He'll get the cemetery done first – that's the difficult bit. Everything else will be easy. The documents have been signed. Bogdan has the diggers ready.

"In fact," thinks Ventham, "what is he waiting for? What would Branson do?"

"Screw it. Let's do it."

Ian switches off the book and, without slowing his run, rings Bogdan.

CHAPTER SIX
The diggers arrive

Every morning, Edwin Ellidge wakes at 6 a.m. and walks slowly to the bottom of the drive at Coopers Chase. When he reaches the main road, he looks left and right, and then walks back. His work done, he is back in his apartment by 6:30 a.m. and usually not seen for the rest of the day. Once, Elizabeth had got up early and met him "accidentally" on his return. His dark shape had reminded her of her happy days in East Germany. He had shaken his head and said, "No need, I've already checked," and they had walked quietly back together.

So, it is Ellidge who sees them first, and lets the other residents know.

Ian Ventham's Range Rover comes in first at 6 a.m. Ellidge sees him pull away from the road and take the track up to the Playfair farm. Bogdan's diggers follow at around 6:20 a.m.

At 7:30 a.m. Ventham drives back down with Karen Playfair – who is about to give a talk to the residents on computers – only to discover that the whole village is outside. Bogdan has just got out of a digger and is about to open the metal gate on to the narrow path to the cemetery.

"Wait a minute." Ron Ritchie approaches Bogdan and shakes his hand. "I'm Ron Ritchie. So, what's this?"

"It's a digger," replies Bogdan.

"Yes, obviously," says Ron. "But what's it for? And don't say digging."

Bogdan sighs and looks at his watch. "You said to not say digging. I don't have other answer."

"This gate only leads to one place," shouts Ron. He turns to stare at the crowd of pensioners behind him and sees his **gang** among them. Joyce is there, carrying a garden chair, and Ibrahim, wearing his yoga clothes. Elizabeth stands at the back, and Ron is surprised to see Stephen next to her in his pyjamas. He's not the only one wearing them.

Even John, Penny's husband, has stopped here on his way to visit her at Willows.

"So, you've come into our village to dig up our nuns," Ron says, turning back to Bogdan.

"Yes," says Bogdan.

Ian Ventham parks his Range Rover next to the digger and steps out. "Good morning, Mr Ritchie," he says. "I'm afraid I need your people to move so that I can do some digging. You've had your consultation. So, if I want to drive on to my land and dig it, then I will."

Joyce turns to the crowd. "Radio Kent says the weather is going to be lovely today," she shouts. "We could all have a picnic."

The pensioners quickly bring chairs, picnic tables, sandwiches, packets of biscuits and cakes. Sadly, it's too early for wine but maybe if they stay here long enough? Soon, there are twenty chairs in front of the gate, with some pensioners having a sleep in the morning sun. Tea is brought out, and photographs of grandchildren are passed around. Karen Playfair is happily chatting to the residents while Ian Ventham sits in his car. As Ventham takes out his phone to call the police, Elizabeth slowly leads Stephen home.

Elizabeth has not told anyone, but Stephen is often confused these days. He talks a lot about his daughter Emily and how she never visits. Elizabeth always listens patiently and does not tell Stephen that Emily is, in fact, his first wife. And although Stephen still writes every day, sometimes it is just to copy something from a newspaper. Elizabeth gives him sleeping pills at night and manages as best she can.

After she has made Stephen a coffee, Elizabeth heads back out, but she does not go back to the crowd. Instead, she follows a path up through the wood and enters the cemetery. Elizabeth knows to look where the action is not happening. Very soon, she hears a sound coming from the trees. The next moment, Bogdan appears with a **spade** over his shoulder.

He heads up the path, nodding to Elizabeth as he passes.

"Bogdan," she says. "I know you have work to do, but I wonder if I can ask you a question."

Bogdan stops his walk and stands the spade on the ground.

"Did Mr Ventham tell you that he wanted Tony Curran murdered?" asks Elizabeth. "After their argument? Did he ask you to help? You have a nice new job now, don't you?"

Bogdan does not look shocked. "Only answer is no," he says. "No, he didn't tell me and no, he didn't ask, so no, I didn't help."

"Can I ask if you put in Tony Curran's CCTV and alarm?"

Bogdan nods. "Sure. Ian gets me to do all that stuff for people."

"So, you could get into Curran's house?" said Elizabeth. "And wait for him? Sorry if I'm being rude, but would Ian Ventham ask you to kill Tony, if he wanted him dead?"

"There are some jobs I do, like fix alarms, tile swimming pools," says Bogdan, smiling. "And other jobs I don't, like kill people."

"I'm sorry for all the questions," says Elizabeth. "Where are you from, Bogdan?"

"Krakow, in Poland. You know Krakow?"

"Yes. It's a beautiful city. I went there for business many years ago. My name is Marina," Elizabeth adds, shaking his huge hand.

"Marina?" repeats Bogdan. He smiles again. "That's my mother's name."

"How lovely!" says Elizabeth. She is not proud of herself, but she has seen the tattoo on his arm.

"I hope to see you again, Bogdan," she finishes and starts walking back down the hill.

"I hope to see you, too, Marina."

Bogdan turns back to the cemetery and starts to dig with his spade. Why not? He can work without the digger. He starts at the very top, where the **graves** lie under the shadow of the trees and the earth is soft.

As he digs, he thinks about Marina. He has seen her before in the village, but people don't usually talk to him. They don't even notice him, and that's OK.

Bogdan's spade finally hits something hard, but it is not a **coffin**. He reaches down and moves the earth. The thing below it is hard and white. Beautiful, actually, thinks Bogdan, before he realizes what it is. Then he sees more of them.

This was not part of Bogdan's plan. If there are bones, they should be in a coffin, not here. He kneels down and realizes he is on the **lid** of a coffin, which is impossible. A body cannot escape from a coffin. Using all his strength, he breaks off part of the coffin's lid. Inside is another skeleton. So, there is one skeleton below the lid, which is grey and yellow, and another on top of it, which is cloud-white.

Bogdan needs thinking time, but, unfortunately, he does not have it because he can hear the sound of police cars approaching to clear the picnic. Bogdan pulls himself out of the grave and quickly refills it.

"Ian will tell me what to do," he thinks.

Ventham gets out of the police car feeling calm, happy even. The officers have had a quick talk with him. He'll come back tomorrow. The residents will soon lose interest. He'll give them something else to complain about – fire some of the restaurant waiters, maybe, or stop grandchildren using the pool for safety reasons. Then they'll be thinking "what cemetery?"

But at that moment, he sees the priest from the consultation standing there in his black clothes and white dog collar, talking to the residents like he owns the place. Ventham moves quickly towards him, and points his finger in Father Mackie's face.

"If you weren't a priest, I'd knock you down!" Ventham shouts. He pushes the older man backwards. Mackie holds on to Ventham's T-shirt for balance, and Ventham falls at the same time. Both men hit the ground together. Donna, Karen and Joyce pull Ventham off the priest, and a group of residents, including Ron and Ibrahim, hold him. Another group stands around Father Mackie, who sits on the ground looking confused.

"Calm down, Mr Ventham!" shouts Chris Hudson. "And go home before I arrest you for hitting a priest!"

Ian Ventham nods unhappily. He shakes his head slowly and sadly at Chris Hudson. "Something isn't right here," he says. Then he walks slowly away, thinking. "Where's Bogdan? Bogdan's a good man. He's Polish. He's too lazy. They all are. I'll talk to Tony Curran. But did Tony lose his phone? Where's Tony?"

Ventham reaches the Range Rover. His dad will be angry – he's only borrowed it. Ian is frightened and starts to cry. He does not want to go home. He searches his pockets for money and then falls.

Ian Ventham is dead before he hits the ground.

CHAPTER SEVEN
Witnesses to a murder

Joyce

You must not speak badly of the dead, I know that. But you know those people who feel the world belongs to them? They say you see it more and more these days, but some people were always awful. Not many, of course, but always a few. So, yes, I'm sorry that Ian Ventham is dead, but there's another way to look at it. On any day, lots of people die, and I would prefer it to be Ian Ventham than a kind person. I've seen many people die, and I've cried a lot of tears. But I haven't cried any tears for Ian Ventham.

And now, I have to go and help ***solve*** *his murder.*

"So, we're all witnesses to a murder," says Elizabeth, putting photographs of Ventham's body on to a table. "Which is wonderful, of course. The cause of death was fentanyl given by **injection** very shortly before death. I got this information from one of my sources – a man who's able to read the emails of Kent police."

"What's fentanyl?" asks Ron.

"It's a drug," says Joyce. "They use it in hospitals to help with pain."

"If it was given to him just before his death, then we're all suspects in his murder," says Ibrahim.

Joyce claps her hands. "Oh, wonderful!"

"There were sixty-four residents at the gate, including ourselves," Ibrahim tells them, "and then you have DCI Hudson and PC De Freitas, Bogdan and another digger driver, and Karen Playfair, who was meant to be talking to us about computers. And then, of course, Father Matthew Mackie. That's seventy suspects. How can we bring the list down? Well, it must be someone who was standing close to him in order to give him an injection. Also, many of the residents are not very fast at getting around. Take out the wheelchairs and walking sticks, and you have thirty names, ourselves included."

"So, who wanted him dead?" says Ron. "And did the same person kill Curran and Ventham?"

"Funny to think, isn't it," says Joyce, "that we know a murderer?"

"It's great," agrees Ron.

"Well, we'd better get started," says Ibrahim.

Back at the police station, Chris Hudson is speaking to the murder team. "We know the injection of fentanyl was given by someone who was there that morning. So we already know our killer and maybe Tony Curran's killer, too."

Donna thinks about the Thursday Murder Club. They had all been standing around Ian Ventham, but she could not see any of them as his murderer.

"Ian Ventham wasn't a popular man," continues Chris. "He had a lot of difficult and possibly criminal business deals, and he was married but dating other women. So, tell your loved ones they won't be seeing much of you for a while."

Loved ones. Donna realizes she has not thought of Carl for forty-eight hours. Soon, it will be ninety-six hours, and then a week. Really, why had she left London? What happens when these murders are solved and she is back doing paperwork?

"And I still need the information on the phone number that called Curran," finishes Chris.

Which reminds Donna of something that she's been meaning to check.

Handsome DI Terry Hallet puts up his arm, and Chris realizes he could never wear a T-shirt that tight. Chris is sure that, one day, Terry will have his office. Terry has four children and a happy marriage. Chris wishes he was Terry, but who knew what really happened at home. Maybe there is some sadness in Terry's life that Chris does not know about – it is unlikely, but Chris holds on to this thought.

"I've got something you're going to like," Terry says. "It's a car that took twelve minutes to travel the half mile between the two speed cameras on either side of Curran's house. The time taken means it had to stop for ten minutes somewhere in between – just enough to murder someone."

"And you've checked the registration number?" asks Chris.

Terry nods and smiles. He puts a piece of paper in front of his boss.

"Well, this is good news," says Chris. "Are you sure about

these timings?"

Terry Hallet nods. "That's our killer, surely?"

Chris has to agree. It's time to have a chat.

Chris and Donna sit on plastic chairs with cups of coffee, watching Jason Ritchie flying and jumping across the ice as he practises for *Celebrity Ice Dance.* When he was a boxer, Jason Ritchie had been beautiful to watch – a strong, brave athlete. But, after more falls than they can count, it is clear that he cannot ice dance.

When Jason finishes and steps off the ice, Chris walks forward and holds out his hand. It is the first time that Jason has noticed the two officers.

"Have you got five minutes, Jason?" asks Chris. "We've come a long way to see you."

Jason nods, and the three of them sit down. He starts to untie his ice **skates**.

"Thought I might see the two of you again," he says. "Have you got another photo for me?"

"What were you doing at Tony Curran's house on the day he was murdered?" asks Chris.

"I don't have to answer that," replies Jason, pulling off the first skate.

"But you agree you were there?" says Donna.

"Our speed cameras caught you. It gave you just enough time to stop at Curran's for ten minutes," says Chris.

"I've got a question, too," says Donna. "On the day that Tony

Curran was murdered, did you call him?"

"I don't remember, I'm afraid," replies Jason, his head still down.

Chris nods. "Because a mystery number phoned Tony Curran three times on the morning of his death – one we could not find through the phone company. But, luckily, it was a number that you had written down and given to PC De Freitas."

Jason pulls off the second skate and nods. "That was silly of me. Well, it sounds like you've got yourselves a mystery there. Now, I'm going to head back."

Jason stands. Donna and Chris do, too. "I wonder if you'd like to come to Fairhaven Police Station and give us your fingerprints and DNA? Just so that we can rule you out?" asks Chris.

"I think our time is finished here, don't you?" says Jason, starting to climb the stairs to the changing rooms. Chris and Donna watch him disappear and then sit back on their plastic chairs and stare over the ice.

"So, what do you think?" asks Chris.

"If he did it, why did he leave a photo with him in it next to the body?" says Donna.

Chris shakes his head. "Maybe some people are just stupid."

"He doesn't seem stupid," says Donna.

"Agreed," says Chris.

CHAPTER EIGHT
Where is Johnny?

Bogdan has seen where Marina lives and feels sure she will know what to do with the bones. He felt it as soon as he met her. He has brought her flowers from the wood and tied them the way his mother used to tie them.

Apartment 8. He rings the bell, and a man's voice answers. This surprises Bogdan.

Bogdan walks into the apartment to see an old man in pyjamas.

"I come looking for Marina?" says Bogdan. "I think maybe she live here but maybe another apartment?"

"Marina?" says Stephen. "Of course, of course. I don't know where she is, but she won't be long. Let's make some tea, shall we? Do you play **chess** at all?"

When Elizabeth comes in some time later, she finds her husband and Bogdan quietly playing chess together. Stephen is staring hard at the board.

"He beat me, Elizabeth," says Stephen.

Elizabeth looks at her husband, who has a huge smile on his face. He is very happy to have found someone to play chess with, and she falls in love for the thousandth time.

"It's Marina, darling," she says.

"He fixed the light in my office, too, Elizabeth," says Stephen.

"It's Marina–" Elizabeth repeats.

"I call you Elizabeth. Is OK," says Bogdan. He stands up and puts a hand on her arm. "You have a beautiful home and a wonderful husband. Now, can I show you something?"

"Of course, Bogdan," she replies.

"I can trust you?"

She looks deep into his eyes. "Of course you can trust me."

"Can you and I go to the cemetery? This evening when it's dark? There's something I want you to see."

Jason Ritchie sits in a corner, finishing a very tasty lunch in the Black Bridge – now called Le Pont Noir. He does not know what to do.

He is surprised by the changes in this place. It has really become upscale with its expensive menu and furniture, soft lighting and beautifully designed grey-black sign. All its dark corners and rough edges are gone.

"Mine have, too," thinks Jason.

He is thinking about the photograph that lies on the table in front of him. He would feel a lot safer with a gun, and, twenty years ago, getting one would be easy. But the gang has gone now.

Ever since he sat down, Jason has been trying to remember exactly where in the pub Tony Curran had shot that young drug dealer – a boy sent from a London gang who were looking for new markets. Jason thinks it might be by the fireplace. He remembers the bullet had gone through the wall and straight into the side of Turkish Johnny's car. Johnny had been really angry, but it was Tony, so what could he do?

Turkish Johnny. Jason has been thinking about him a lot. He's sure Johnny took the photograph that was left by the body. He always had a camera on him. Had Johnny come back? Had Bobby Tanner come back? Was Jason next on their list?

The boy had died in the end. He'd tried to sell Steve Ercan drugs on the seafront. Steve stayed near the edges of the gang but was never really part of it. He told the kid to try to sell his drugs at the Black Bridge, knowing that he would find Johnny and Tony there. After the kid was shot, a cab driver Tony liked to use for these situations drove the body away and hid it. Then the cab driver was shot, too, because Tony thought you could never be too careful.

That was the end of things for Jason, and all of them. It was no longer about making money, friends and fun, but guns and dead bodies. He'd realized it all too late.

Bobby Tanner left soon after. His younger brother, Troy, had died on a boat, bringing drugs in from Europe, and Johnny disappeared immediately after the cab driver was shot.

Those days were gone, and Jason could not be more glad about it. There was nothing left of them here in this new, upscale Black Bridge. But where was Bobby? Where was Johnny? How could he find them before they found him?

Well, he probably knows the answer to that. He has always known it. He takes out his phone and calls his dad.

CHAPTER NINE

A night in the cemetery

"I got the photo on the morning of Curran's murder," Jason explains to Ron. "There was no stamp. It was pushed through the letter box."

Father and son are drinking bottles of beer on Ron's balcony.

"And you recognized it?" asks Ron.

"Not the photo," replies Jason. "I've never seen it before. But I recognized that it's Tony Curran, Bobby Tanner and me in the Black Bridge, where we used to drink. I took you there once when you visited me, do you remember?"

Ron nods and looks at the photo. "And where was the money from?"

"Drugs, of course," replies Jason. "It was always drugs in those days. The police have got this photo."

"You know I have to ask, Jason. Did you kill Tony Curran?"

Jason shakes his head. "I didn't, Dad, and I would tell you if I did, because you know there would be a good reason. I need to find Bobby Tanner or Johnny. I'm sure it's one of them. I can understand someone else leaving the photo by Tony's body as a **red herring**, but why send it to me, too? Or did Bobby or Johnny want me to know that they did it?"

"And you want our help to find them?"

"That's why I'm here, isn't it?"

Ron nods. "I'll call Elizabeth."

It's difficult to smoke in a sauna but Jason is trying hard. Opposite him and his father sit Elizabeth, Ibrahim and Joyce in their towels.

"So, I got this photo," Jason is explaining, giving it to Elizabeth. Ibrahim has wrapped it in clear plastic. "But there's no note, nothing. And I thought that maybe Tony had found it and was thinking, 'He's a famous boxer and TV celebrity, got lots of money and criminals around him. If he gives me twenty grand, I won't go to the newspapers.' So I decided to ring him."

"Was Tony Curran the sort of man who might do that?" asks Elizabeth.

"He's the sort of man who might do anything. So, first of all, I got a new phone, a cheap one, in town. I rang him once, then tried again, and then one more time. He didn't pick up. After that, I came here for a quick drink with Dad and Joyce, and that's when we saw Curran arguing with Ventham.

"After that, I drove down to Tony's house. His car was on the drive, so when there was no answer, I thought, 'He must be able to see me on his CCTV and doesn't want to talk.' I understood – too many secrets – so I went home. A bit later, someone from the old gang rang me and said someone had found Tony dead at home. I went cold because I'd got the photo that morning and, in the afternoon, Tony was killed. Then the police learned I'd been to Tony's, and they knew I'd rung him. I can see that makes me a strong suspect."

"They do have a lot of reasons," agrees Ibrahim.

"And you're here to see if we can find your old friend for you?" asks Elizabeth.

Jason nods. "My dad says that you're just as good as the police – and probably better. And it's old friends. There's Bobby Tanner, but also the man who took the photo. His name's Turkish Johnny. He went back to Cyprus just after the shooting."

"I have some good sources in Cyprus," says Elizabeth.

"So, what do you think?" asks Ron.

"Well," says Elizabeth. "I feel that this is a problem that you made for yourself, Jason, which came from crime and drugs. And I'm not happy about that. But you're Ron's son, and I believe you're probably right. I think we can find Bobby Tanner and Turkish Johnny, and quickly. And despite what you've done, I'd like to catch a murderer. Do we agree?"

"We agree," say Joyce and Ibrahim.

"Thank you," say Ron and Jason.

"But I do hope you're telling the truth," adds Elizabeth. "Because we *will* catch this murderer, even if it's you."

Austin holds on to Ibrahim's arm and steps down on to the lid of the coffin as Bogdan shines a torch on him. Then, Austin looks up at Elizabeth and smiles. "This takes me back, Lizzie," he says. "Remember Leipzig?"

Elizabeth smiles back. She certainly does. Joyce smiles too

because she has never heard Elizabeth be called Lizzie before.

"What do you think?" asks Ron, drinking a can of beer.

"Well, from the colour, I think these bones have been down here for some time," replies Austin. "What's the date on the grave?"

"Eighteen seventy-four," reads Joyce.

"They've not been here that long. Forty, fifty years, perhaps. Not a hundred and fifty."

"So, someone has **buried** another body on top of the coffin?" says Ibrahim.

"Definitely," says Austin. "You have a mystery to solve here."

"Another nun perhaps?" Elizabeth asks. "Are there any dark clothes?"

"Nothing on this one," says Austin. "I'm going to take a few bones with me, if you don't mind. I'll look at them in the morning."

Bogdan looks at Elizabeth. "So, we tell police now?"

"I think we should wait until Austin reports back to us," says Elizabeth. "Now, shall we all go back to Joyce's for a nice cup of tea?"

"That would be wonderful!" says Austin, putting a handful of bones on the edge of the grave before climbing out.

"You lead the way, *Lizzie*," says Ron, and finishes his can of beer.

"Now, we can do this in one of two ways," says Elizabeth. "You

1874

can shout at us, or you can just accept what has happened and we can get on with it. Your choice."

Chris cannot speak for a moment. He looks up to Joyce's ceiling then down to the floor. "You . . . dug up a body?" he says, finally. "And then you asked an expert to look at the bones? And you did this without reporting it to the police?"

"Elizabeth, this isn't pretending to be a nun," says Donna. "You could go to prison for this."

"A nun?" says Chris.

"It doesn't matter," replies Donna, quickly.

"I knew you'd react like this," says Elizabeth. "Now, please can we move on? We didn't want to take up your time until we knew for sure what the bones were."

"Imagine if they'd been cow bones," agrees Ibrahim. "We'd look like silly old things then!"

"Anyway," continues Elizabeth, "my expert looked at them and yes, they're human bones. A male who was once shot in the leg, although we don't know if that killed him. He died sometime in the 1970s. As soon as we knew that, we decided to contact you. Think of the money and time we've saved you!"

Chris is trying to find an answer. Donna decides to find one for him. "Joyce, you were a nurse. You knew that they were human bones."

"Well, yes," admits Joyce.

"This is a serious crime. How can you be so stupid?"

"Enough. If you're going to arrest us, then arrest us," says

Elizabeth. "You can take us to the station and question us all night. You won't get any answers because none of us will speak. Or you can believe us when we say we were trying to help you. Then, tomorrow, you can dig up the bones yourselves and send them to your own experts, so we'll all be happily in the same place. And we can spend the rest of this evening enjoying our wine and talking about why someone buried a body on this hillside sometime in the 1970s."

Chris looks at Donna.

"We can also discuss whether that same person has just murdered Ian Ventham to keep it secret," adds Elizabeth.

"So, you think the same person murdered two people?" says Chris. "With fifty years between them?"

"It's an interesting question, isn't it?" asks Elizabeth. "That it might be someone who was here in the 1970s and is still here now. So, what do you think about the priest, Father Mackie? Was he here when this place was a convent?"

"It's Doctor Mackie, not Father Mackie," says Donna. "We've been checking his past. He's not a priest. He was a doctor in Ireland who moved over here in the nineties. He **retired** from medicine fifteen years ago and lives in a house in Bexhill."

"That's confidential, of course," says Chris.

"You're quite safe with us," says Elizabeth. "Can we just forget about us digging up the bones and share our information?"

"I think we've shared quite enough for one day, Elizabeth," says Donna.

"Oh, really," says Elizabeth. "But you haven't even told us about the Tony Curran photograph yet. We had to find that out for ourselves."

"As a way to say sorry," says Ibrahim, "perhaps you'd like to know who took the photograph?"

Chris sighs. "I would like to know that, yes."

"It was a man called Turkish Johnny," says Ron. "And I think if you find Turkish Johnny or Bobby Tanner, you'll find Tony Curran's killer."

"What about your son?" asks Chris. "Has he explained his phone calls to Tony Curran on the morning of the murder, or why his car was in the area when Curran was killed?"

"Yes," says Elizabeth. "We're happy with what he's told us."

"I'll ask him to call you and explain, don't worry," says Ron. "But shall we try to find this Turkish Johnny and Bobby Tanner?"

"Let the police do that," says Chris.

"I'm sorry, but I'm afraid we can't just let you do that," says Elizabeth.

"Would you like some wine?" says Joyce.

Chris sits back in his chair and lets her pour it. "If this ever gets back to my boss, I will arrest you and put you in prison myself, I promise."

"Chris, no one will ever find out," says Elizabeth. "You know what my job used to be?"

"Well, no–"

"Exactly."

CHAPTER TEN
A trip to the florist's

Chris Hudson is drinking beer. He loves real fires, and they have a nice one burning in Le Pont Noir. He's never eaten here because who would he eat with? Once, he had dreamed of being married and having children – a boy and girl. They would sleep quietly while he and his wife were downstairs – she would be reading a book while he read case notes. But he has none of that, just a fire in a bar where there's no one to talk to, and an apartment where no one ever cooks. On the way home there, he decides, he will buy a Dairy Milk chocolate bar – a really big one.

He's sure that Mackie is guilty of Ventham's murder. Why was he pretending to be a priest if he was a doctor? But did these bones change things? Had there been two murders, one to protect the other? If this was true, then Mackie had not done it. He did not leave Ireland until the nineties.

Chris's thoughts move to Tony Curran's murder. Jason Ritchie had rung him earlier and explained the calls and the car. If Jason had been lying, then he had done it very well. But then he would, wouldn't he?

They still could not find Bobby Tanner. He'd disappeared after leaving Amsterdam. Maybe he was in Brussels, still **smuggling** and fighting. Or maybe he had been back to visit Tony Curran for some reason? Something connected to Bobby's brother drowning in that boat full of drugs, perhaps?

And then the new name, Turkish Johnny. Chris had found plenty in the police files about him. His real name was Johnny Gunduz. He had left the country in the early 2000s after becoming a suspect in the murder of the cab driver in the Black Bridge shooting. Everything kept coming back to that one night in this bar.

Had Johnny come back?

Chris finishes his beer and looks one more time at the fire. He should probably go home.

Joyce and Elizabeth are sitting in Casa Café in Folkestone. Peter Ward has just taken half an hour off from selling flowers in his very successful **florist's** shop to buy them both a coffee. Peter is greying and smiling, and is relaxed in the way of a man who has made good decisions in his life.

But this has not always been true because Peter Ward is actually Bobby Tanner. Or perhaps Peter Ward has left Bobby Tanner behind. That is what Elizabeth and Joyce have come to find out.

Elizabeth puts the photo on the table between them, and Peter picks it up, smiling.

"The Black Bridge," he says. "We had some good nights in there. Where did you get this?"

"Two places," says Elizabeth. "One was sent to Jason Ritchie, and one was found by Tony Curran's body."

Peter Ward nods. "I read about Tony," he says. "It was always going to happen."

"You've never seen this photograph before today?" says Elizabeth.

He shakes his head.

"Well, that's either good news for you or good news for us," says Elizabeth. "Either Tony Curran's killer doesn't know where you are, or you killed Tony Curran yourself and we haven't had to come all the way to Folkestone for nothing."

"Not that it's for nothing," says Joyce, smiling. "We're having a lovely day."

"The police think that Jason killed Tony Curran," starts Elizabeth. "And perhaps he did. What do you think, Bobby?"

Peter Ward puts up a hand. "Peter, around here, please."

"What do you think, Peter?" asks Elizabeth.

"I don't see it," says Peter Ward. "Jason looks tough, but he's very gentle inside. He couldn't hurt anyone."

Elizabeth puts the photo back down on the table. "So, if not Jason, then who? Perhaps you? Or perhaps Turkish Johnny."

"You know about the Black Bridge murder?" says Peter. "The boy Tony shot in the Black Bridge? Then Johnny shot the taxi driver who hid the body?"

"We know that, yes," agrees Elizabeth. "Johnny disappeared back to Cyprus."

"Well, it wasn't that simple," says Peter Ward. "Someone told the police about Johnny – we don't know who. The police went to

Johnny's apartment, but he had already gone, taking a hundred grand of Tony's drug money with him. Tony went crazy."

"Did Tony try to find Johnny?" asks Elizabeth.

"Of course. He went to Cyprus a couple of times, but he couldn't find out anything. So, I'm guessing you haven't found Johnny either?"

Elizabeth shakes her head.

"How did you find me anyway? I really don't want to be found by anyone if Johnny's back in town, leaving photos of me next to bodies."

Elizabeth picks up her coffee. "Woodvale Cemetery, where they buried your brother, Troy. I got the CCTV of the cemetery, thanks to a friend. You visited on the twelfth of March and the seventeenth of September – his birthday and the date of his death. Both times, a Folkestone florist's van was parked outside with your name, address and telephone number on it."

Peter lifts his hands and gently claps. She smiles.

"She's very good, Peter," says Joyce.

"I see that," says Peter. "So, no one else can find me?"

"Not unless I tell them where you are," says Elizabeth.

"And is that something you're likely to do?"

She sits forward. "Not if you come and see us tomorrow, sit down with Jason and the police, and tell them what you've just told us."

Joyce

Well, that was good fun. Firstly, I've never been to Folkestone before.

I think I have two things to write about. Why was Peter Ward a florist? And who did he think killed Tony Curran?

Peter (that is what I'll call him) told us he left Fairhaven soon after his brother died and went to Amsterdam, where he met a gang from Liverpool and started smuggling drugs back into the UK. They bought a farm, where they grew flowers, and had three lorries a day coming through Zeebrugge Port in Belgium, carrying drugs hidden in the flowers to England. But then they made a mistake – a florist in Gillingham accidentally received drugs in with their roses, and reported them to the police. The police quickly arrested everyone in the smuggling gang. Luckily, Peter and another young man, who were managing the farm, saw the police coming and hid until they left.

Peter had made a bit of money and learned a lot about flowers. So he decided to start his own florist's in Folkestone, but now the lorries only deliver flowers.

So, that's a nice story. And just to prove things to Elizabeth, Peter showed her the CCTV of himself in his shop on the day Tony Curran was killed. I think this rules him out. Peter's sure that Turkish Johnny is our murderer because Tony had told the police about him shooting the cab driver. I think that would be enough of a reason. So, that's Bobby Tanner. It's time for bed now.

CHAPTER ELEVEN
Donna meets Penny

Donna and Chris are sitting in Joyce's apartment with cups of tea. Opposite them are Jason Ritchie and Bobby Tanner, whom detectives all over England have not been able to find. Elizabeth will not share how she found him.

Elizabeth tells them she and Joyce have both seen information proving that Bobby was not in Fairhaven when Tony Curran was murdered. Bobby will tell the police everything he knows and then be allowed to disappear back to his life.

"A bit more than a hundred grand," says Bobby. "Johnny had it at his apartment. He kept money safe for Tony. Tony went to Cyprus several times but never found him. Nothing was the same after that. Jason, you went off, didn't you? Started doing TV."

Jason nods. "I couldn't do it any more."

"But surely someone saw Johnny," asks Donna. "If he came back to town recently?"

Bobby thinks about this. "There's not too many faces left from those days."

"It's hard to know who Johnny would go to if he needed a place to stay," agrees Jason.

Bobby looks at Jason. "Unless . . ."

Jason looks back at Bobby, then nods. "Of course, of course . . ." He immediately starts writing a text.

"Are you going to share this?" asks Elizabeth.

"It's just someone me and Bobby need to talk to," says Jason. "Someone who'll know."

His phone pings. He looks down, then turns to Bobby. "He can meet us at two. That OK for you?"

Bobby nods and Jason starts replying to the message. "Only one place for it, don't you think?"

Two hours later, Jason and Bobby are having lunch at Le Pont Noir, just like old times. But, of course, not like them at all.

"So, what are you doing now? Racing horses? Flying to the moon?" asks Jason.

Bobby Tanner shakes his head and smiles. "I'd never tell you, even if you guessed."

"Are you happy, though?" Jason asks.

Bobby nods.

"Good, you deserve it," says Jason.

"We both do," agrees Bobby.

"Well, we do and we don't," says Jason.

They have just finished a bottle of one of Le Pont Noir's very expensive wines.

"You think he'll know?" asks Bobby.

"If Johnny's been here, he'll know. That's where Johnny would stay."

"I can't drink at lunchtime any more," says Bobby. "Can you?"

"We're old men now, Bobby," agrees Jason. "Time for another bottle, though?"

They agree that they do have time for another bottle. And then Steve Ercan walks in.

After their last meeting at Coopers Chase, Elizabeth had told Donna that she wanted her to meet someone. She then led her to Willows, the nursing home attached to Coopers Chase. They had walked into the room, and Elizabeth had said, "Constable De Freitas, I'd like you to meet Detective Inspector Penny Gray."

Penny was lying in bed with tubes running from her nose and wrists. An old man sat on the other side of her, reading a book.

"Take a seat, Donna," said Elizabeth. "I want you two to get to know each other."

Elizabeth told Donna about Penny's career and how strong she had once been in her mind and body. She described how Penny had fought the men who wanted to stop her just because she was female and angry, and how she had never risen higher than Detective Inspector despite her abilities.

Finally, Elizabeth put her hand on Penny's. "She was trouble, Donna. That's why she enjoyed looking over the old cases. She could finally be the boss."

After they left, so different in age but shoulder to shoulder and taking the same steps, Elizabeth had turned to Donna and said, "You know better than me, of course, but not all the fights have been won?"

"I don't think they have, no," Donna had agreed. They had continued in silence out through the front doors of Willows, happy to be breathing the air of the outside world.

Back at home – was this really home now? – Donna can see on her phone that Carl has a new girlfriend, but Donna is not really thinking about Carl any more. The visit to Penny has made her sad. There are many reasons why Donna would like to solve these murders, and she adds making Detective Inspector Penny Gray proud to her list.

CHAPTER TWELVE
Two confessions

Joyce

Everyone's been wondering what will happen to Coopers Chase now that Ian Ventham is dead. Then Elizabeth "accidentally" met Ian's wife, Gemma, in a shop in Robertsbridge. She was with a good-looking younger man and didn't seem very sad. We all agreed that she deserved a bit of happiness.

She's also made a lot of money because she's sold Coopers Chase to a company called Bramley Holdings. Of course, we've tried to find out as much as we can about Bramley Holdings, but even Joanna and Cornelius couldn't find anything.

But that name – it's reminding me of something, only I can't think what. Bramley, where have I heard that before? Yes, I know there are Bramley apples, but it's not that. It's something else, something important.

"Lovely?" repeats Gordon Playfair, laughing. "This place? It's an old house with bits falling off it, for an old man with bits falling off him."

"We've all got bits falling off us," says Elizabeth. "You don't hear too much noise from the village?"

"Never hear anything," replies Gordon. "It could still be the nuns down there."

"You should come and visit us," says Joyce. "There's an

upscale restaurant, and a swimming pool and sauna. You can do yoga, and all sorts of exercise classes."

"I used to go down there in the old days," Gordon replies. "Just to get things and have a chat. The nuns were good fun when they weren't praying."

Elizabeth nods. "You met with Ian Ventham on the morning he was murdered, didn't you?"

"Unfortunately, yes. My daughter Karen wanted me to speak to him. She wants me to sell. Why wouldn't she?"

"And what was discussed?" asks Elizabeth.

"Same offer, same rudeness. I never liked Ventham. Karen knew it wasn't working, but Ventham kept going – he tried to make me feel guilty about the kids – but I wasn't going to change my mind."

"And how was it left?" asks Elizabeth.

"He told me he was going to get my land one way or another."

"And what did you say to that?" asks Joyce.

"I said, 'Over my dead body.' Anyway, I've been made another offer, and I'm going to take it now that Ventham isn't around any more."

"That's good," says Elizabeth.

Gordon Playfair smiles. "Now, can I ask, is this just a friendly call, or is there something I can help you with?"

"I'm glad you asked," replies Elizabeth. "We were wondering if you have any **memories** of this place from the seventies?"

"I have lots of memories," replies Gordon Playfair. "I might even have some photo **albums** if they would help, but I must warn you there are a lot of sheep. What is it that you're looking for?"

Joyce

So, we told Gordon Playfair about the body and wondered who might be buried there after all those years. The offer on his land, by the way – it's from the same company, Bramley Holdings! Trying to remember that name is making me crazy.

I asked Gordon what he was going to do with the money, and it's going to go to his kids, but he'll have enough left to buy himself somewhere nice. So we're going to give him a guided tour of Coopers Chase in a few days and see if he likes it. Won't that be fun? Gordon isn't handsome in the usual way but has strong farmer's shoulders.

Anyway, back to the bones. Gordon understood now why we wanted to hear his memories of the 1970s. We wanted to look at any photos he'd taken on those journeys down the hill all those years ago. The album started with pictures of Gordon's wedding, and then the babies, and then picture after picture of sheep.

And then, just as the wine and the fire and the sheep were making us sleepy, we reached the final photos in the album. There were six of them, all black and white, and all taken at Christmas at the convent. It was the fifth photo that interested us – a group picture. At first, you couldn't really see it – we've all changed a lot in fifty years. But we looked, and we all looked again.

And now, Elizabeth has a plan.

There is still a small **confessional** in the chapel at the heart of Coopers Chase. It is usually used as a cupboard now, but Joyce and Elizabeth have emptied it out and cleaned it.

Elizabeth has done a lot of interviews in her life, mostly without lawyers. Whatever worked quickest. Her ways were never violent, though – the mind was the important thing. Always try the unexpected and wait for them to **confess** all. Like inviting a priest to a confessional. But what if it did not work? She had been wrong about Ian Ventham murdering Tony Curran, hadn't she?

But Matthew Mackie was different. This was a man who had fought with Ian Ventham, who was never here yet was in a photo taken in this chapel, who was a priest but not a priest. He was a man who had brushed over his footsteps.

The chapel is cold. Elizabeth shivers and stares at Mackie through the darkness.

"I don't want your forgiveness, or God's. I just want to have someone hear my **confession** before I die. I know there are rules, even in a confessional, so you must do what you need to do with this information. I killed a man. I was living in an apartment in Fairhaven at the time. I invited him home, and he attacked me. I fought back, and I shot him in the leg and then watched him die. I managed to pull his body to my car, and then I drove up to the cemetery here. You know it?"

"I know it, yes."

"I knew it because I worked here once for a short time. I took my spade and chose a grave right at the top, and I dug until I hit the lid of a coffin. Then I pulled the body over the ground to the grave. Finally, I dropped it in. I filled the grave and prayed. Then I walked back to my car, put the spade in the back, and drove off."

"I understand," says Father Mackie, softly. "But I don't believe a word of it, Elizabeth."

Mackie was surprised when he got the call from Elizabeth, asking if he would listen to a confession. And even more for it to happen in the old confessional in the chapel at Coopers Chase. He had always known that his life would lead him back there one day.

Mackie had seen Elizabeth before, he was sure. At the consultation meeting and on the day of the murder. "What is she hiding?" he thought when he got the call. "What thing has she done that was so awful she could no longer hide it?" She had seen his priest's dog collar, that was it. It often made people want to tell their secrets. So, back to where it all began and all ended. But Elizabeth could not possibly know that, could she?

"Not a word?" Elizabeth replies now. "That was a lot of detail, Father Mackie. The date. A bullet in the leg, the grave."

"Elizabeth, you didn't work here in 1970."

"Mm," she says. "You did though. I've seen the pictures."

"I did, yes. I've sat here before. And I've sat where you are, too."

Elizabeth decides to start turning the knife. "You sound like a man who wants to talk. Have my words brought back memories? Are you worried that I know something?"

Matthew Mackie laughs sadly. "Well, yes, maybe I would like to talk. I've always wanted to. So while we're both here in God's house, why don't you start somewhere, and I'll join in when I can."

"Shall we start with Ian Ventham?" asks Elizabeth. "Why did you kill him?"

CHAPTER THIRTEEN
A surprising date

Joyce

I am getting worried. Elizabeth has been gone too long – more than two hours. I'm writing this while I'm waiting for Donna to arrive. She's very angry with us, and very worried, and so am I. I always thought Elizabeth could not be hurt by anyone. I hope I'm not wrong.

Sister Margaret Anne
Margaret Farrell, 1948–1971

Elizabeth takes Matthew Mackie's hand and holds it. She looks out over the wall to the fields, the hills, the trees, the birds. The cemetery really is a beautiful place.

Then the peace is broken by the sound of running feet. Elizabeth looks at her watch. "This will be Joyce and the police," she says. "I told them that if I wasn't back in two hours, they had to come and get me."

"Was it that long?"

Elizabeth nods. "There was a lot to say, Matthew. And now, you'll have to tell it all again when the police finally get up this hill."

Elizabeth can see Chris Hudson now, running heavily towards them. She waves and she can see he's glad – both that she is still alive and that he can now stop running.

Matthew Mackie sits in an armchair of the Jigsaw Room. The Thursday Murder Club are in their usual seats, and Chris and Donna have brought in a couple of chairs from the lounge.

"I had only just arrived from Ireland," Mackie tells them. "I really was a priest back then. It was the same as now; very beautiful, very quiet – there were a hundred nuns here, but you wouldn't know it. The head nun, Sister Mary, was very strict, and the other nuns were really frightened of her. But it was also a place of work. I'd walk around, talking about God, and take confessions."

"And you lived here?" asks Chris.

"There were some rooms at the back of the convent. They were nice. I wasn't allowed visitors, of course. That was the rule."

"A rule you followed?" asks Donna.

"At first, of course. But things change. I'd met Maggie very early on. She cleaned the chapel. You know when you look into someone's eyes for the first time and the whole world changes? That was Maggie. She used to come to confession but say nothing. We just sat there, our hearts beating hard. Slowly, we fell in love, and she started to visit me in secret in my rooms."

"Can I just check," says Chris. "Maggie is Sister Margaret Anne?"

"She is. I knew we had to get out. It would be easy enough. I'd find a different job. Maggie could nurse. But it was much harder for young women in those days. Because then, Maggie realized she was expecting a baby, and even worse, she told someone in the convent who told Sister Mary. Sister Mary called Maggie to her office and told her she was to be sent back to Ireland the next day. Maggie went to the chapel that night and hanged herself. She took her life and the life of our child."

Father Mackie looks up at the other six people in the room. "That's my story. And nothing was ever fine again."

"So is Maggie's grave up on the hill?" asks Ron.

"That was the deal I made," says Mackie. "I was to leave and go back to Ireland, where I retrained as a doctor. And in return for keeping quiet about Maggie, I asked them to bury her in the cemetery here, where it's so peaceful. I knew Maggie didn't want to go back to Ireland."

"And Sister Mary agreed?" asks Donna.

"It looked better for her, too. Fewer questions. I went back home, and that's where I stayed until I heard that Sister Mary had died. She's buried up in the cemetery, too. When I heard the news, I left my job, packed a suitcase and came back to stay as near as I could to Maggie."

"And that's why you did everything you could to stop the bodies being moved?"

Mackie nods. "It was the only thing I could do for Maggie. It was all I had to say sorry and to say 'I still love you' for the only love I ever knew, and for our baby boy or girl. But it's a boy I've always carried in my heart. I called him Patrick."

"I'm sorry to say this at this time, Father," says Chris, "but this gives you a very good reason for killing Ian Ventham."

"But I didn't do it," replies Mackie. "Maggie would never have forgiven me if I'd killed Ventham. I've always done what Maggie would want because one day, I'm sure I'll see her again, and my little boy, and I want to do that with a pure heart."

With his tour of Coopers Chase finished, Gordon Playfair is sitting with Ibrahim, Elizabeth and Joyce on Ibrahim's balcony. Gordon has a beer, and the others are drinking wine. Chris and Donna have returned to Fairhaven. Matthew Mackie has gone home to Bexhill, and Joyce has promised to visit him. She loves Bexhill.

"I could get used to this place," says Gordon. "There seems to be a lot of drinking here."

"Always," agrees Ibrahim.

The phone rings, and Ibrahim gets up to answer it. "That was Ron," he says when he returns. "He wants us to join him in his apartment. Jason is with him and has something to tell us."

"So, Bobby and I had lunch in the Black Bridge," Jason tells them, lifting a bottle of beer to his mouth. "It felt like we sort of trusted each other. We'd both changed into better people, but we still couldn't be sure that the other hadn't killed Tony. Then, our source came in and we asked him straight – has Johnny been back? Have you seen him?"

"And had he seen him?" asks Elizabeth.

"He had," says Jason. "Johnny came over three days before Tony was murdered and left the day he died. He was angry with Tony for telling the police about him."

"So, why did Johnny send you the photograph, Jason?" asks Ibrahim.

Jason shakes his head. "I think he just wanted us to know it was him who killed Tony. Johnny was like that. Whatever he did, he had to let you know. And my address must be easy to find as I'm a celebrity. But now, I have something else to tell you."

Jason takes out his phone and turns it to show them a photograph on a dating app. "I think I know who killed Ian Ventham," he says. "And tomorrow, I'm planning to meet them."

Having spent an enjoyable morning getting ready, Karen Playfair is now alone for a moment, sitting in an armchair. She is shaking her head, thinking of the excitement of preparing for the **date** and then the date itself. Because Karen has met some strange men through dating apps, but this was the first time that someone had accused her of murder.

The face pinged on to her phone yesterday evening. Jason Ritchie, the boxer and TV celebrity. "Well, why not?" she had thought. "This is better than usual."

He had messaged, and she had replied, and suddenly there they were, eating a salad.

Karen moves in her armchair and picks up something from

the coffee table. It is the Coopers Chase newsletter, *Cut to the Chase*.

Back to the date. They had talked a little. Some wine arrived, and that was when Jason mentioned Ian Ventham. Karen immediately realized this was not a date and felt stupid. But then, it got even worse when Jason started asking her questions like, hadn't she been there on the morning Ventham was killed? Yes, she had. Wasn't her dad refusing to sell his land to Ventham? Yes, he was, but look, here's our soup. Jason kept going. Surely, if her dad sold to Ventham, then she would get some of the money? Well, yes, but why not just say what you want to say, Jason?

And so he had, and it was almost funny when he told her the police had been looking for someone who was at Coopers Chase in the 1970s – even if she was a child – and still there now. And didn't Karen have good reasons – she wanted the money? Ventham was in the way of Karen making millions. And fentanyl was used, and that could be bought if you understood the internet? Didn't Karen work with computers? Jason was sure he had solved the case and was going to get a confession. He did not expect Karen to laugh in his face and explain that she worked for a school, looking after their computers, and had no better understanding of the internet than he did. She also said that she lived in one of the most beautiful places in England, and, yes, she would like a million pounds but would rather be there with her dad happy, than in some new home in a town where he felt sad and uncomfortable.

Karen remembered how disappointed Jason had looked. He knew that she was telling him the truth. He had said sorry and offered to leave, but Karen had wondered if they should not try to enjoy the rest of their lunch. Because what if they got together, she said. Wouldn't this be the greatest "and how did you meet?" story of all time? Which made them both laugh and got them talking, and suddenly they were having a lovely, long, wine-filled lunch.

And this was why Jason had asked her back here to his father's for another drink and to explain to his dad.

Just at this moment, Ron Ritchie walks in with Jason and a bottle of white. Jason sits down next to Karen and hands her her wine. He has been lovely to her since accusing her of murder.

Karen puts *Cut to the Chase* back down on the table and, as she does, she sees a photograph. She picks it up again, just to be sure.

"You all right, Karen?" says Jason.

"You said the police wanted someone who was here in the seventies, who's still here now?" she asks, slowly and carefully.

Ron looks at the photograph, but his brain won't take it in.

"You're sure?" he asks.

She nods. "It was a long time ago, but yes, I'm sure."

Ron's mind is racing. This can't be. He puts the wine down on the coffee table.

"I need to go and talk to Elizabeth," he says.

CHAPTER FOURTEEN
"The gang's all here"

Elizabeth leaves Stephen sleeping. Bogdan will be coming here after work for a game of chess. She hopes they will both be there when she returns. She will need to be with people.

She walks out into the cold evening. It's nearly the end of summer, and the skies are getting dark earlier. Soon, it will be autumn. How many more autumns for Elizabeth? How many more years of putting on comfortable boots and walking through the leaves? She must enjoy it while she can.

She sees Ron coming towards her with a serious face, and Ibrahim waiting by the door with a file under his arm. How handsome and well he looks. Ibrahim will be the last of them, she thinks. The last tree in the forest.

"How do I even begin?" thinks Elizabeth.

They walk along the corridor with Ron carrying a couple of chairs. Then, there's the sound of the front door opening once more, and Joyce is suddenly hurrying up behind them. They walk silently until they reach the door. Elizabeth knocks, as she always does, and then opens it. And there he is, the man who Karen Playfair recognized after all those years.

The same book is open at the same page. He looks up and seems unsurprised to see the four of them.

"Ah," he says, "the gang's all here."

"The gang's all here, John," agrees Elizabeth. "Do you mind if we sit?"

John nods and puts down his book as Ron sets down the chairs.

"How shall we do this, John?" asks Elizabeth.

"It's your decision," replies John. "I've been waiting for that knock since the moment I did it. I do wish you'd taken a bit longer though. What was it, in the end?"

"Karen Playfair saw that photo of you, Ron, and the injured fox. She recognized you from when you were a vet and you looked after her dog when she was six," says Ibrahim. "She says she would never forget your kind eyes."

Elizabeth is in her usual seat next to Penny's bed. "Who's in the grave, John?"

With his eyes shut, John turns his face to the ceiling. "It was back in the early seventies," he starts. "I went to a farm to look at a horse that was in a lot of pain. The owner didn't want to shoot her, which I understood, so I gave her an injection and that ended things. We went inside and got chatting. He was a very lonely man. He had no family to help him on the farm and no money. It was very wild and lonely up there, or that's how it seemed to me that day, and I wanted to leave. But then, I realized that this man was very unhappy. If he had been an animal, he would have been screaming. And, so, I reached into my bag, and I gave him an injection – the same one I'd given the horse."

"You put an end to his suffering?" asks Joyce.

"That's how I saw it."

"So, you had to bury him, this farmer?" asks Elizabeth.

"Yes, but I didn't want to bury him on his farm because I knew it would be sold and someone might dig him up. And then I thought of the cemetery here. It wasn't on farmland, and no one was going to buy a convent. So I got my spade and drove up here one night to bury him. And that was it, until one day, forty years later, I saw an advertisement for this place."

"And here we are," says Elizabeth.

"And here we are. I persuaded Penny it would be a lovely place to retire to, and I wasn't wrong. But I also wanted to keep an eye on things here and be close by if the worst happened."

"Which it did, John," says Joyce.

"I'm too weak now to dig the body back up. So while we were holding him, I quickly gave Ventham an injection, and seconds later, he was dead. I know what I did is terrible in every way. Terrible. And from that moment, I've been waiting for you to come."

"How were you suddenly able to **inject** Ventham with fentanyl, John?" asks Elizabeth.

John smiles. "I've had it a long time – since I was a vet. I've always known I might need it. If they ever wanted to move Penny."

"You know we have to tell the police?" Elizabeth says.

"I know."

"But, while it's just us, can you explain a few things? I think we both agree that Penny probably doesn't hear what happens in this room?"

John nods.

"But I think we also agree that maybe she does?"

"Maybe," agrees John.

"And if she does, then why would you do that to her? Why put her through that?"

"Well, I–"

"You wouldn't, John, that's the truth," says Elizabeth.

Ibrahim sits forward. "John, you said that killing Ian Ventham was a terrible thing to do, and I believe you mean that. But now you're asking us to believe you did that just to save yourself? I'm sorry, but it doesn't sound true. There's only one reason for what you did."

"Love, John," says Joyce. "Always love."

John looks at the four of them with an unreadable face.

"I sent Ibrahim to look at one of Penny's files this morning," says Elizabeth.

Ibrahim takes the file from under his arm and hands it to Elizabeth. She opens it on her knees. "Shall we get to the truth?" she says. "As you know, Penny kept files of all her unsolved murders. It wasn't allowed of course, but that was Penny. She took copies of everything–"

"Because maybe, many years later, she would see something or think of something," finished Joyce.

"Anyway John," continues Elizabeth. "After Karen Playfair

recognized you, I started thinking, and I wanted to check one final thing in one of the files."

John's eyes are on Elizabeth as she begins to read.

"There was a case in Rye, in 1973, when Penny was a young police officer. It was about a girl called Annie Madeley. You remember Annie Madeley, Penny?"

Elizabeth looks over to where her friend is lying.

"Annie was stabbed during a **burglary**. She died in the arms of her boyfriend. The police found broken glass on the floor where the **burglar** got in, but nothing was stolen. The burglar was surprised by Annie. He picked up a kitchen knife, stabbed her, and ran. That's what's in the police file, anyway. But Ron wasn't happy when he read it."

"It just sounded wrong, John," says Ron. "A burglar in the middle of the day on a busy street? On a Sunday, when people are at home?"

Elizabeth looks over at Penny. "You knew it was wrong, too, didn't you?" She picks up the sponge and wipes Penny's lips.

"We started looking at it months ago, John. I was surprised that Penny had never shown it to us. I read the report on the knife wound, and it didn't seem right to me. In fact, I think it was the first thing I ever asked you, Joyce?"

"It was," remembers Joyce.

"I described the wound and asked her how long it would take for someone to die, and Joyce said around forty-five minutes – this didn't fit with what the boyfriend had said. He had chased the burglar then run back to hold Annie in his arms and ring the police. The knife hadn't cut an artery, so I asked Joyce if someone with a bit of **medical** training would be able to stop the blood and save Annie, and what did you say, Joyce?"

"I was certain about it," replies Joyce. "You know that, too, John, with your training."

"The boyfriend, Peter Mercer, had been a soldier," continues Elizabeth. "So he definitely had medical training. He'd had to leave the army for medical reasons. He knew what to do to save her, but he didn't. But that's not how the investigation went. I'd like to say that things were different back then, but I'm sure he would get away with it today, too. They searched for the burglar but with no luck. Poor Annie Madeley was buried, and the world kept turning. We were reading all about this case, but then things happened – Tony Curran and Ian Ventham, the body in the cemetery. We put the case to one side while we had a real murder in front of us."

"But we know that's not the end of the story, don't we, John?" says Ron.

"So, I asked Ibrahim to find out what the medical reasons were for Peter Mercer leaving the army," continues Elizabeth. "Can you answer that question, John?"

John buries his head in his hands, pulls them down his face and looks up. "Because he was shot in the leg?"

"It was just that, John."

Elizabeth pulls her chair nearer to Penny, takes her hand and speaks to her quietly.

"Nearly fifty years ago, Peter Mercer murdered his girlfriend, and then disappeared. Everyone thought he'd got away with it, but it's really not that easy to get away with murder, Penny, is it? Sometimes, punishment is just around the corner, just like it was for Peter Mercer one dark night when you went to visit him. Had you just seen too many of those cases, Penny? Were you tired of them, and tired of no one listening?"

"When did she tell you, John?" asks Joyce. "When she was first ill?"

John starts to cry and then nods slowly. "She didn't mean to tell me. You remember how she became, Elizabeth? She started saying strange things, and then the present seemed to disappear, and her mind went further and further back, and she started telling me stories from years ago. Some were not real, some were from when she was a child, or when we first met. Things we'd laughed about. I knew I was losing her, and I wanted to hold on to her for as long as I could, you understand?"

"We all do, John," says Ron.

"So, I kept her talking. But then . . ." John looks at his wife. "But then it was stories I didn't know. Secrets. Small things at first, like a bit of money she'd stolen as a child. But there was something right at the back of it all, a final lock on a final gate."

"The worst secret of all?"

John nods. "I came in one morning about two months ago, and she was sitting up. It's the last time I remember her doing that. And she saw me, and she knew me. She asked me what we were going to do, and I said, 'Do about what?' and she started to tell me. You know I couldn't let people find out what she'd done, Elizabeth? You know that? I had to try something."

They sit silently, listening to the sound of Penny's heart machine. It was all that was left of her, like a light going on and off far out to sea.

Then Elizabeth says, gently, "Here's what I think we should do, John. I'm going to get the others to take you home while I stay with Penny for a while. It's late. Have a sleep in your own bed. If you have letters to write, then write them. I'll come with the police in the morning. I know you'll be there. We'll go outside now so that you can say goodbye."

The four friends step outside, and Elizabeth watches through the glass of Penny's door as John holds his wife in his arms. Then she looks away.

When she opens the door again, John is putting on his coat.

"Time to go, John."

The three friends go with John, leaving Elizabeth with Penny. She is holding her friend's hand.

"So, did anyone get away with anything, darling?" Elizabeth asks. "Tony Curran didn't, did he? Everyone thinks that Johnny killed him, although I have an idea I must discuss with Joyce. And Ventham – well, you know John has to pay for that. I'll take the police there in the morning and they'll find his body, we both know that. He knows how to make it peaceful, doesn't he?"

She touches Penny's hair. "And what about you, you clever girl? Did you get away with it? I know why you did what you did. I see the choice that you made. I don't agree with it, but I see it."

Elizabeth puts Penny's hand back on the bed and stands.

"I know what John did while he was holding you, Penny. I saw him inject you, so I know you're going, and this is goodbye. Darling, I haven't spoken about Stephen recently. He's not at all well, and I'm trying my best, but I'm losing him bit by bit. So I have my secrets, too."

She kisses Penny's cheek.

"I'll miss you so much. Sweet dreams my friend."

Then Elizabeth leaves Willows and walks out into the darkness.

The lights in Donna's apartment are low, and she's playing Stevie Wonder. Chris is happy and relaxed with his shoes off. Donna pours him a glass of wine and then another for her mother, who is sitting next to Chris on the sofa.

"Seriously, you could be her sister, Patrice," says Chris. "And that's not because Donna looks old!"

Patrice laughs. "Madonna said you were funny."

Chris looks at Donna. "Your real name is Madonna?"

"If you ever call me that, I'll shoot you," says Donna, turning off the music and putting on the TV. "Jason Ritchie is on *Celebrity Ice Dance*," she says. "Shall we watch it?"

"Sure, sure," says Chris, but he is thinking about other things. He turns to Patrice. "So, what do you do for work?"

"I'm a teacher," replies Patrice.

"Are you?" says Chris. "Teacher," he thinks, "who sings and loves dogs." Patrice could be his perfect woman.

Suddenly, Donna's phone pings. She looks down at it.

"It's Elizabeth. She wants to know if we're free tomorrow morning?"

"She's solved the case, of course," jokes Chris.

Donna laughs and hopes everything is OK with her friend.

CHAPTER FIFTEEN
A game of chess

Elizabeth is out late, but Bogdan and Stephen have not noticed. Bogdan is staring at the chess board and thinking hard about how to move next. He looks up quickly at Stephen. How does this man play so well? If Bogdan isn't careful, he is going to lose. And Bogdan does not remember the last time he lost.

"Bogdan, can I ask you a question?" says Stephen.

"Always," says Bogdan. "We are friends."

"Because I know I've got you in trouble and you're concentrating."

"Stephen, we play, we talk. They are both special." Bogdan moves his castle forward. He looks up at Stephen, who is surprised but not yet worried.

"I just wanted to know the name of the man who was killed," Stephen says, "– the first one. The builder?"

"Tony," says Bogdan. "Tony Curran. What's your question?"

Stephen moves his queen. "Well, it's just this. From everything I've heard, I think you killed him. Elizabeth talks to me, you know."

Bogdan looks around the room for a moment, and then back at Stephen. "Sure, I killed him. It's a secret though. Only one other person knows."

"Of course, it's a secret. No one will hear it from me. But why? Not money, surely?"

"No, not money. You have to be careful with money. You can't let it be your boss. No, it was simple. I had a friend, Kazimir. He drove a taxi. One day, Kazimir saw Tony do something he shouldn't."

"What did he see?" asks Stephen.

Bogdan stares down at the board. "He saw Tony shoot a boy from London. A drug thing. The taxi company was run by man named Turkish Johnny. Tony was Johnny's boss. And Johnny was Kazimir's boss."

"So, Johnny killed your friend?"

"Johnny killed my friend, but Tony told him to. I don't care. Is same thing."

"It is. We agree here. So, what happened to Johnny?"

Bogdan pulls back his castle. The last move was not good, but never mind, these things happen.

"I kill him, too. Soon after. At first, I thought Kazimir had run away to home. But then Johnny start telling people what he did. Johnny is stupid, not like Tony. Johnny, he ask Kaz to drive him to woods. He has to bury something, and he needs help. They walk into woods, they dig and dig, for whatever Johnny needs to bury. He was hard worker, Kaz, you would like him very much. So, then Johnny shoot Kaz. One shot, and buries him in the hole."

Stephen concentrates on the board, and Bogdan worries he has lost him, but he has learned that you must be patient with Stephen. And he is right.

"So, you decided to do something about it?" the older man suddenly asks.

Bogdan nods. "I tell Johnny I need to speak to him. Don't tell

Tony, don't tell the others. I say a friend works in Newhaven port and there might be some money for him, and is he interested? And he's interested, so we meet at the port at 2 a.m. with a man called Steve Ercan, and he comes with us. Steve know Kazimir, was also his friend. So, we get in little boat and Johnny, he is stupid, he just think about money. We sail, sail, sail, and water is rough, and I'm telling him plan, that we use this little boat to **smuggle** people and drugs. Then I take out a gun, and I tell him kneel down, and I say, 'You killed Kazimir' so he know why, and I shoot him. I take his cards and keys. We put stones in his pockets and throw him in sea. We go back to Newhaven, and then we drive to his apartment. We take his passport and pack suitcase full of clothes. There is a lot of money – drug money – and we take this, too. I knew some of the money was Tony's, so I'm glad to take it."

"How much money?" asks Stephen.

"It was like one hundred grand. I send fifty grand to Kazimir's family. The rest I give to Steve. He's a good man, no problem with him. Then I drive Steve to Heathrow, and he take flight to Cyprus on Johnny's passport. No one looks. Easy. Then Steve fly back to England on his own passport. I call the police – not say my name – and tell them Johnny killed Kazimir. They go to his apartment."

"And they find his passport and clothes are gone?"

"Yes. So they check ports and airports and find out he's gone back to Cyprus. They look for him there, but he's disappeared.

They leave it with the Cypriot police. Everyone forgets in the end."

"You took your time with Curran, though," says Stephen.

"Always waiting for the best time," agrees Bogdan. "So, a couple of months ago, Ian Ventham asked me to put in CCTV and an alarm for Tony, so I did it wrong. Nothing recording. And I thought 'Now is the time, I can get in house,' so I got keys made, no one can see me."

Bogdan suddenly attacks one of Stephen's pieces. Stephen nods and moves it, but he is not feeling hopeful. "Clever," he says.

"Just after I do it, there's a ring at the door, but I stay calm, no worry."

Stephen nods again. "But what if they catch you? Elizabeth will solve it, if she hasn't already."

"I know, but I think she will understand."

"I do, too," agrees Stephen. "But the police would be different."

"If they catch me, they catch me, but I gave them very good red herring I think."

"A red herring? And how did you do that?"

"Well, when we went to Johnny's apartment that night, one of the things we took was a camera, so . . ."

But Bogdan stops speaking when they hear a key in the lock. Elizabeth is back late from wherever she has been. Bogdan puts a finger to his lips, and Stephen does the same.

"Hello, boys." Elizabeth kisses Bogdan on the cheek and then hugs Stephen tightly for a long time. As she does, Bogdan moves his queen for the last time.

"Checkmate," he says. "I win again."

Elizabeth lets Stephen go, and he smiles at the board and at Bogdan. Stephen reaches out and shakes Bogdan's hand. "He's a clever player, this one, Elizabeth. A very clever player."

Elizabeth looks down at the board. "Well played, Bogdan."

"Thank you," says Bogdan, and starts preparing a new game.

"Well, I have an interesting story for you both," says Elizabeth. "Can I make you a cup of tea, Bogdan?"

"Yes, please," says Bogdan. "Milk. Six sugars."

Elizabeth walks into the kitchen. She thinks about Penny, surely dead by now? That was how it ended, in an act of love. Then she thinks about John, lying down for his final sleep. He had looked after Penny, but at what cost? Is he at peace now? She thinks of Annie Madeley and everything she has missed. Everyone has to leave the game. Once you're in, there is no other door but the exit. She reaches for Stephen's sleeping pills and then changes her mind.

Stephen and Bogdan begin another game. Elizabeth turns back to the kitchen, and neither man sees that she is crying.

CHAPTER SIXTEEN
Joyce

Sorry I haven't written for a while. It's been very busy around here. But I have an apple pie baking in the oven, and I thought there might be a few things you would want to know.

They buried Penny and John last Tuesday. It was a rainy day, and that seemed right. There were a surprising amount of people there, some who knew Penny from work. It had been in the newspapers, about Penny and John. They hadn't got the whole story correct, but they were near enough.

Elizabeth wasn't at the funeral. I'm afraid I think Penny was right, and I'm glad she did it, but that's not something I would tell anyone else. Elizabeth is much cleverer than me, and I know she has thought about it more, but I don't think she can disagree with what Penny did. But I do think Elizabeth must be sad at the secret. There were these two great friends with their mysteries, yet all that time Penny was the biggest mystery of all and Elizabeth never knew.

Penny killed Peter Mercer, and she kept it from John all her life until she became ill. And once John knew, he had to protect her. That's love, isn't it? Because Peter Mercer murdered Annie Madeley, John murdered Ian Ventham.

The police haven't yet found Turkish Johnny, by the way, but they're still looking. Chris and Donna have come to visit a few times. Chris has a new lady friend, but is being quiet about it for now, and Donna won't talk about it. Chris says they'll catch Johnny one of these days, but Bogdan came here to fix my shower the other day, and he says Johnny is too smart for that.

My feeling is that Johnny is too easy as a suspect. So, Johnny came over and killed Tony because he had told the police about him, but why would Tony do that? Because Johnny helped him to hide a murder? It doesn't seem very likely.

No, the only person who is too smart to be caught is Bogdan.

Don't you think he killed Tony Curran? I do. I'm sure he had a good reason, and I look forward to asking him. But not until he's fixed my window, because he might not like the question.

I'll check the pie in a minute. Shall we get on with more pleasant matters?

Gordon Playfair sold his farm, and there are already diggers up there. I heard from Elizabeth that he got £4.2 million for his land. He said goodbye to the house he'd lived in for seventy years and packed his things into a van. Then, he drove it 400 metres down the hill and unpacked them at a nice two-bed in Larkin Court. Bramley Holdings gave him the apartment as part of the deal, which brings us to another bit of news.

Bramley Holdings? I now know why I remembered the name. When she was very small, Joanna had a little toy elephant that was pink with white ears and that she kept with her at all times. Its name was Bramley.

So perhaps you can see what's happened?

When we took Ian Ventham's financial file to Joanna and Cornelius, they had looked over his accounts. They liked them so much that Joanna decided to buy Coopers Chase from Gemma Ventham. So, isn't that exciting?

Joanna's company owns the whole place. She came to see me about it and we talked, and I said I didn't think this was the kind of business that they usually bought, and she agreed. But she said they wanted to try new things. She did add that there was plenty of money to be made, but she told me she had another reason, too. Which I'll tell you now.

She sat on the sofa that she had bought me and, taking my hand, she said,

"Remember when you moved in here, and I told you it was a mistake? I said it would be the end of you, sitting in your chair with other people who were just waiting for their days to end? I was wrong. It was the beginning of you, Mum. I thought I would never see you happy again after Dad died. Your eyes are alive, your laugh is back and it's thanks to Coopers Chase, Elizabeth, Ron and Ibrahim. And so I bought it – the land, the whole development."

And a couple of things you'll want to know. The cemetery is staying. Joanna says they'll make enough money from Hillcrest, so the Woodlands development has been cancelled. The graves are also now protected in law, so Matthew Mackie doesn't need to worry.

The other day, Elizabeth invited Matthew for lunch, and he came without his dog collar. We told him that Maggie was safe now, and you could see that he was nearly crying, but he didn't. Instead, he just asked to visit the grave. We walked up to the cemetery with him and waited by the gates as he walked through them and knelt down at the grave. And then the tears did come, as we knew they would when he saw the gravestone. I had watched a couple of days ago as Bogdan had gently cleaned it and added "Patrick, 1971" to it. There's really nothing that Bogdan can't do.

This morning, Elizabeth rang me to tell me that someone has put a very interesting note under her door. How exciting! But, of course, it's Thursday, so I must go to the Jigsaw Room. I was worried that after Penny's death we would stop meeting, but that's not how things happen around here. Life goes on, until it doesn't. The Thursday Murder Club goes on. Strange notes are pushed under doors, and murderers fix windows. I hope it continues for a long time.

And right on time, the oven pings and my apple pie is ready. I'll let you know how everything goes.

During-reading questions

CHAPTER ONE

1 Why does Elizabeth ask Joyce about the stabbing?
2 Why was the Thursday Murder Club started, who is in it, and where and when do they meet?

CHAPTER TWO

1 What does "having none of it" mean, do you think?
2 What is The Woodlands consultation about, and what does Ian Ventham want to do when this part of the development is finished? How does he plan to do this?

CHAPTER THREE

1 Why does Elizabeth go to see Penny, and why is John there?
2 Why does Donna pretend to tie her shoe?

CHAPTER FOUR

1 How did Tony Curran use to make his money?
2 Why does Jason ask for a copy of the photo?

CHAPTER FIVE

1 Why is it important that the Thursday Murder Club learns the times that Ian Ventham left Coopers Chase and Tony Curran died?
2 Who is Bobby Tanner? Why do the police need to speak to him?

CHAPTER SIX

1 What does Bogdan find in the cemetery?
2 Why does Ian Ventham become angry at the end of the chapter?

CHAPTER SEVEN

1 How did Ian Ventham die?
2 Why do Chris and Donna go to interview Jason Ritchie?

CHAPTER EIGHT

1 Why is Stephen happy to meet Bogdan?
2 Why was the cab driver shot?

CHAPTER NINE

1 Why has Jason gone to see his dad?
2 How old are the bones? Why is this important?
3 What information do the Murder Club and the police share?

CHAPTER TEN

1 Who is Peter Ward, and how did Elizabeth find him?
2 How did Peter Ward become a florist?
3 How do the Murder Club know that Peter Ward is not a suspect in Curran's murder?

CHAPTER ELEVEN

1 What do Bobby Tanner and Jason decide to do?
2 Why didn't Penny rise above Detective Inspector, do you think?

CHAPTER TWELVE

1 What has Elizabeth learned from Gemma Ventham?
2 What does "over my dead body" mean, do you think?
3 Why does Elizabeth tell Matthew Mackie that she killed a man in Fairhaven, do you think?

CHAPTER THIRTEEN

1 Who is Sister Margaret Anne, and why is she buried in the cemetery?
2 "This gives you a very good reason for killing Ian Ventham," Chris tells Matthew Mackie. What is this reason?
3 How and why does Jason arrange to meet Karen Playfair? Is it a successful meeting?

CHAPTER FOURTEEN

1 Who does John tell the Murder Club is buried in the cemetery? Why does he say this person is there?
2 Who is really buried there?
3 Why does Elizabeth say "I'll miss you so much" when she says goodbye to Penny?

CHAPTER FIFTEEN

1 Why does Bogdan admit the truth to Stephen, do you think?
2 Why did the police think that Turkish Johnny went to Cyprus?
3 Why does Elizabeth start to cry?

CHAPTER SIXTEEN

1 Why didn't Elizabeth go to the funeral, do you think?
2 Who bought Coopers Chase, and why?
3 What is in the "very interesting note", do you think?

After-reading questions

1 Will Bogdan get away with his crime, do you think?
2 What does the story say about old people, do you think?
3 What was Elizabeth's job, do you think?
4 Is *The Thursday Murder Club* mostly a serious book, do you think, or a comedy (written to make people laugh)? Give reasons for your answers.

Exercises

CHAPTERS ONE AND TWO

1 Match the words with their definitions in your notebook.

Example: *1 – d*

1 stab	a the time when you are not working any more
2 nursing home	b when you meet and go out with your boyfriend or girlfriend
3 retirement	c when an employer tells someone that they must leave their job
4 cemetery	d to push a knife into a person's body
5 fire	e a place where people live when they are too old or ill to look after themselves
6 shiver	f a place where dead people are buried
7 date	g when your body shakes because you are cold or frightened

CHAPTER THREE

2 Write the correct verb form, *present perfect* or *past perfect*, in your notebook. Are there any sentences where both are possible?

1. Elizabeth arrived at Ibrahim's apartment very early. She **has / *had*** rung him the night before with the news about Tony Curran.
2. After visiting Ibrahim, she **has / had** immediately come to see Penny.
3. Donna **has / had** placed the tea on a desk. She reaches down, pretending to tie her shoe.
4. He **has / had** been to retirement villages before and this lovely, peaceful development is not what he was expecting.

CHAPTERS FOUR AND FIVE

3 Who is thinking this, do you think? Who are they thinking about? Write the correct names in your notebook.

1. Oh, I hope she's excited to see me. It's so nice of Elizabeth to organize this! *Joyce is thinking about Joanna.*
2. This is great. Now I won't be bored any more. How did they get me on the case?
3. Why are they showing me photographs and what do they want from me?
4. If I ask him to come outside, he might tell me the truth.
5. I must tell her what time I saw Ventham leave.

CHAPTER SIX

4 Which word is closest in meaning? Write the correct words in your notebook.

1	resident	*guest* / owner / driver
2	digger	spoon / car / spade
3	nun	waitress / priest / police officer
4	grave	hole / grass / stone
5	coffin	hill / sky / box
6	lid	box / cover / bottom

CHAPTER SEVEN

5 Complete these sentences with the correct form of the verb in your notebook.

1 I've ***seen*** / **saw** many people die and I've cried a lot of tears.
2 Well, it must be someone who **was standing** / **stands** close to him in order to give him an injection.
3 He was married but **dates** / **dating** other women.
4 The time **took** / **taken** means it had to stop for ten minutes somewhere in between – just enough to murder someone.
5 What were you doing at Tony Curran's house on the day he was **murdered** / **murdering**?

CHAPTER EIGHT

6 Are these sentences *true* or *false*? Write the correct answers in your notebook.

1 Bogdan knew that Elizabeth had a husband. ...*false*.....
2 Stephen is happy to have someone to play chess with.
3 It is easy to get a gun now.
4 The boy was killed because he tried to sell drugs in the area where Tony Curran controlled them.

CHAPTER NINE

7 Make these sentences reported speech in your notebook.

1 "I got the photo on the morning of Curran's murder," Jason explains to Ron.
Jason told Ron that he got the photo on the morning of Curran's murder.

2 "It was always drugs in those days," replies Jason.

3 "Did you kill Tony Curran?" asks Ron (to Jason).

4 "Was Tony Curran the sort of man who might do that?" asks Elizabeth (to Jason).

5 "How can you be so stupid?" asks Chris (to Elizabeth and Joyce).

6 "Would you like some wine?" says Joyce (to Chris).

CHAPTERS TEN AND ELEVEN

8 Complete these sentences in your notebook, using the words from the box.

florist's	grand	suspect	gang
	smuggling	drugs	

1 Peter gave up crime and started selling flowers in a *florist's*.

2 Johnny left England after the police made him a .... for the murder of the cab driver.

3 Johnny left and took one hundred .... of Tony's money.

4 They were arrested for .... into England.

5 Peter and Jason wanted to leave the .... after the shooting in the Black Bridge.

CHAPTERS TWELVE AND THIRTEEN

9 What happened here? Match in your notebook.

Example: *2 – c*

1 Coopers Chase	**a** Gordon used to go down and visit the nuns here.
2 The Playfair farmhouse	**b** Matthew Mackie tells his story to the police and the Murder Club.
3 The confessional	**c** The Murder Club look at photo albums with Gordon Playfair.
4 The Jigsaw Room	**d** Elizabeth meets Father Mackie and tells a lie about a crime.
5 The chapel	**e** Maggie hanged herself.
6 Ron Ritchie's apartment	**f** Jason takes Karen back there and she reads *Cut to the Chase.*

CHAPTER FOURTEEN

10 Write questions for these answers in your notebook.

1 *Who is in the grave?*

Annie Madeley's boyfriend, Peter Mercer, is in the grave.

2 So I could keep an eye on things here.

3 I killed him with an injection.

4 Because he had been a soldier.

5 Because he was shot in the leg.

6 She told me when she became ill.

CHAPTER FIFTEEN

11 **Look at Bogdan's speech on page 91 and 92, from "I tell Johnny. . ." to "I'm glad to take it." Find the mistakes in Bogdan's English and correct them in your notebook.**

CHAPTER SIXTEEN

12 **Match the two parts of these sentences in your notebook.**

Example: *1 – c*

1 Gordon Playfair	**a** because she didn't want him to get away with murder.
2 Elizabeth didn't go to the funeral	**b** to protect Penny.
3 Penny killed Peter Mercer	**c** moved to Coopers Chase.
4 John killed Ian Ventham	**d** of Matthew Mackie's son to the gravestone.
5 Joanna's company bought Cooper's Chase	**e** because Penny kept the secret from her.
6 Bogdan added the name	**f** so that it wouldn't be sold and the cemetery would never be built on.

Project work

1 Imagine you are DCI Chris Hudson. Write five questions for an interview with John Gray about the killing of Ian Ventham. Then write John's answers.

2 Write a newspaper report about the murder of Tony Curran.

3 "His dark shape had reminded her of her happy days in East Germany" (Chapter Six). What was Elizabeth's job, do you think? Write her job title and a description of the things that she had to do.

4 Make a presentation about the problem of drug smuggling gangs in England/your own country.

5 Write a page in Penny Gray's diary for the day she killed Annie Madeley's boyfriend.

Essay questions

1 How did the Thursday Murder Club help the police solve the three murders? Could the police have solved the murders if the Murder Club hadn't helped them, do you think? (500 words)

2 Stephen and Joyce decide not to tell the police about Bogdan. Why do they make this decision, do you think? Is it ever possible to kill for the right reasons? (500 words)

3 Do you feel sorry for Ian Ventham? Why/Why not? Give reasons for your answers. (500 words)

4 ". . . not all the fights have been won," Elizabeth says to Donna. What is she saying about UK policing, do you think? Do you have the same problems in your country? (500 words)

An answer key for all questions and exercises can be found at **www.penguinreaders.co.uk**

Glossary

album (n.)
a book that you keep photos in

artery (n.)
a tube that carries blood from your heart to other parts of your body

boxer (n.); **boxing** (n.)
A *boxer* is a person who does the sport of boxing. In this sport, two people hit each other while wearing very big, thick gloves.

burglary (n.); **burglar** (n.)
Burglary is the crime of entering a building when you are not allowed to, and stealing things from it. A *burglar* is a *criminal* who does a *burglary*.

bury (v.) past tense: **buried**
to put something in or under the ground

CCTV (n.)
Television cameras inside and around a building that are used to watch the building and protect it from *burglary* or other crime. *CCTV* is short for closed circuit television.

celebrity (n.)
a famous person

cemetery (n.)
a place where dead people are *buried*

chapel (n.)
a small church

chess (n.)
a game for two people that is played by moving pieces with different shapes and names (king, castle, etc.) around a board with black and white squares

coffin (n.)
a long box for a dead body

confess (v.); **confession** (n.); **confessional** (n.)
If you *confess* or make a *confession*, you say that you have done something wrong. In the Catholic religion, people go to *confession* in a church. They tell the *priest* about things they have done that they believe are bad or wrong. A *confessional* is a private place in a church where people go to *confession*.

confidential (adj.)
If something is *confidential*, it is secret and you should not tell anyone about it.

consult (v.); **consultation** (n.)
When you discuss something with the person or group of people that it affects before making a decision about it. *Consultation* is the noun of *consult*.

convent (n.)
a building where *nuns* live and work

criminal (n. and adj.)
A *criminal* is a person who has done a crime. *Criminal* is also the adjective of *crime*.

date (v. and n.); **dating app** (n.)
If you *date* someone, they are your boyfriend or girlfriend, or you might want them to be your boyfriend or girlfriend. A *date* is when you meet and go out with your boyfriend or girlfriend, or with someone who you might want to be your boyfriend or girlfriend. A *dating app* is a computer program on your phone that helps you find a person who you might *date*.

DNA (n.)
DNA is in all living things. It tells us about what each person, animal or plant is like. A person's *DNA* can be used to help the police find out if they did a crime.

drug (n.)
Something that people take to make themselves feel happy, excited, etc. Buying and selling *drugs* is against the law.

expert (n.) someone who knows a lot about a subject

financial (adj.) about or connected with money

fire (v.)
An employer *fires* someone when they tell the person that they must leave their job.

florist (n.)
A *florist's* is a shop that sells flowers and plants. A *florist* is a person who owns or works in a *florist's*.

fox (n.)
A wild animal like a dog. A *fox* has red-brown fur (= hair on its body) and a long thick tail. It usually comes out at night.

gang (n.)
1) a group of friends who often spend time together 2) a group of *criminals* who work together

get away with (phr. v.)
to do a crime or something bad and not be punished for it

grand (n.)
in informal English, one thousand pounds or dollars

grave (n.)
The place in the ground where a person is *buried*. There is usually a large stone there with the person's name on it.

incident (n.)
An event, often something bad or unusual. An *incident room* is a room where the police work to collect information about a crime or accident.

inject (v.); **injection** (n.)
If you *inject* someone or if you give them an *injection*, you put medicine or *drugs* into their body by using a needle (= a very thin piece of metal).

interview (n.)
when you ask someone a lot of questions to learn information about something

investigate (v.); **investigation** (n.)
To try to discover information or the truth about something, for example a crime. *Investigation* is the noun of *investigate*.

jigsaw (n.)
A picture made from many small pieces that you put together again for fun. In this story, the *jigsaw room* is a room where people often do *jigsaws*.

lid (n.)
a hard cover for something like a box or a case

medical (adj.)
connected with illness, medicine, doctors and hospitals

memory (n.)
something that you remember from the past

model (n.)
a very small copy of a real thing, often used to show what it will look like or how it will work

nun (n.)
a woman who is part of a religious group of women who live together

nursing home (n.)
a place where people live when they are too old or ill to look after themselves

pensioner (n.)
A *pension* is money that a person who has finished work or *retired* regularly receives from the government or a company. A *pensioner* is someone who is receiving a *pension*.

ping (v.)
To make a short, high sound like a bell. A phone often *pings* when it receives a message.

pretend (v.)
to make people think that something is true when it is not

priest (n.)
A person who has the most important job in a Catholic church. People listen to the *priest* when they go to church.

pyjamas (n.)
trousers and a shirt that you wear in bed

red herring (n.)
an idea, event, etc. that takes your attention away from something that is important, usually in a crime story or an *investigation*

registration number (n.)
a group of numbers and letters on the front and back of a car, bus, lorry, etc. that give information about when the car, etc. was made and who owns it

resident (n.)
a person who lives in a certain place

retire (v.); **retirement** (n.)
To *retire* is to stop working because you are too old, or because you have a big enough *pension*. *Retirement* is when this happens, or the time when you are not working any more.

rule out (phr. v.)
To decide that someone or something is not the right person or thing for something, or that something is not possible. The police *rule out suspects* in an *investigation*.

sauna (n.)
A special room that is heated to a very high temperature. People sit or lie in it to relax and feel healthier.

share (n.)
One of the equal parts of the value (= how much money something is worth) of a company. *Shares* can be bought and sold to make money.

shiver (v.)
If you *shiver*, your body shakes because you are cold or frightened.

sigh (v.)
to let air out of your mouth slowly and make a soft sound, often because you are a little angry, disappointed or tired

skate (n.)
a boot with a thin metal part on the bottom, used for moving around on ice

smuggle (v.); **smuggler** (n.)
To *smuggle* is to take something, for example *drugs*, out of a place in a secret way. This is against the law. A *smuggler* is a person who does this.

solve (v.); **unsolved** (adj.)
To *solve* a problem is to find the correct answer to it. For example, if you *solve* a murder, you find out who did the murder. An *unsolved* murder has not been *solved*.

source (n.)
A person who secretly gives information to someone else. They are the *source* of the information.

spade (n.)
A *spade* is used for digging. It is a long thin piece of wood or metal with a flat metal part at one end that you push into the ground.

spanner (n.)
a metal tool with a round end that is used to turn nuts and bolts (= small pieces of metal used to hold things together)

sponge (n.)
A *sponge* is soft and has a lot of small holes that water goes into. You use it to wash yourself or clean things.

sprinkler (n.)
a machine inside a building that sends water through the air when there is a fire

stab (v.)
to push a knife into a person's body

suspect (n. and v.)
A *suspect* is a person who the police *investigate* because maybe they did a crime. If you *suspect* something, you believe that something (often a bad thing) is true or will happen. If you *suspect* someone, you believe that maybe they did a crime.

tattoo (n.); **tattooed** (adj.)
A *tattoo* is a picture or some words that have been drawn on your skin and stay there forever. A *tattooed* part of your body has *tattoos* on it.

tile (v.)
A *tile* is a flat and often square piece of stone, plastic or other material that you use to cover a wall, floor, roof, etc. If you *tile* a wall, floor, roof, etc., you cover it with *tiles*.

trade union (n.)
Trade unions try to improve pay, hours and the work place for people who do a certain job.

upscale (adj.)
expensive, fashionable and made for or used by people who have a lot of money to spend

vet (n.)
a doctor for sick or injured animals

witness (n.)
a person who sees a crime or *incident*

Visit **www.penguinreaders.co.uk**
for FREE Penguin Readers resources
and digital and audio versions of this book.